Hidden Talents

David Lubar

A TOM DOHERTY ASSOCIATES BOOK
NEW YORK

This is a work of fiction. All the characters and events portrayed in this book are either products of the author's imagination or are used fictitiously.

HIDDEN TALENTS

Copyright © 1999 by David Lubar

Drawing on page 69 by David Bunde

A Starscape Book
Published by Tom Doherty Associates, LLC
175 Fifth Avenue
New York, NY 10010

www.starscapebooks.com

ISBN: 0-765-34265-0

First Starscape edition: January 2003

Printed in the United States of America

0 9 8 7 6 5 4 3 2

For Ashley Grayson, a man with many talents

ACKNOWLEDGMENTS

It's too bad acknowledgments can't be written after a book is published. While it's easy to remember those who've helped during the writing, the help that comes afterward often arrives in magical ways from unexpected places. To make up for my previous inability to know the future, I'm going to use a bit of this space to thank two special people who were wonderfully helpful and supportive after my first story collection came out—Walter Mayes and Kelly Milner Halls. Thank you both. You know what you've done, and I'm grateful.

Now, let's get back to the past so I can thank all the folks who helped with this book. Joelle and Alison were always there and always honest. Ashley Grayson, as usual, did double duty. Jonathan Schmidt had his hand in the manuscript up to the elbow, helping me turn a sketchy first draft into a real novel. Marvelous Marilyn Singer gave me a great number of wonderful suggestions. She's never shy about pointing out my flaws. Thanks, Marilyn. It takes a true buddy to say what stinks. Thanks to Lorraine Stanton and Laura Johnson for sharing what they know about alternative education.

Acres of thanks and oceans of gratitude to Maura Fadden Rosenthal, who did such a fabulous job creating the interior design of this book.

Special thanks to everyone at NKA for helping me learn to focus on the important stuff.

Finally, thanks to those as-yet-unknown champions who will arrive by surprise after these words have been set in stone. I wish I knew your names.

Nazareth, PA
Winter 1998

Hidden Talents

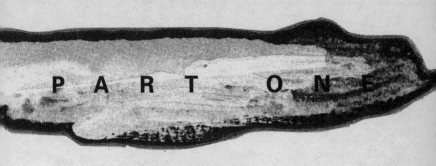

PART · ONE

WELCOME TO EDGEVIEW

OFF THE BUS AND INTO TROUBLE

*A*ll I needed was handcuffs. If my wrists had been chained to the seat, the scene could have been taken straight from one of those movies where they show the bus bringing the new guy to the prison. Of course, there wasn't any need for cuffs on this ride. Fill my pockets with rocks, add a couple more layers of winter clothes—wet winter clothes—and I might push the scale up toward ninety pounds.

The bus driver looked like he weighed three times that much. His wrists were thicker than my neck. He could probably crumple me up like a used tissue and still keep one hand on the steering wheel. No way I was going to cause him any trouble.

So I wasn't in cuffs—but the rest of it felt a lot like going to prison. I was the only passenger on the bus. After a long ride across three counties, we'd reached the main gate at Edgeview Alternative School. A guard out front holding a clipboard waved us inside, then talked with the bus driver for a minute. The two of them reminded me of a pair of dogs who stop for a quick sniff as they pass each other on their way to important doggy missions. I smiled at the thought of the driver wriggling around on his back in the grass.

Once the driver and the guard finished yapping, we rolled through the yard. The building even looked kind of like a prison—big, cold, gray stone, all wrapped up with a high brick fence. Edgeview was the sort of place where people kept broken machines, old tires, and other stuff they didn't need. Yeah, this was a place for things nobody wanted. End of the trip. End of the line. No way I could pretend it wasn't happening.

As the bus stopped near the front door of the building, I noticed all the windows had that dead look of glass filled with wire—the type of windows they use in a gym or a warehouse. A man slipped out from behind the door and walked stiffly down the steps. I got the feeling he'd been watching from inside for the bus to show up so he wouldn't seem like he was waiting. At first, I thought he was real old. As he got closer, I realized he wasn't that much older than my parents—he just moved like he was ancient. He was wearing a dark suit with a bow tie. I never trusted anyone with a bow tie. I didn't trust anyone without a bow tie, either, but I especially didn't trust people who wore them.

The driver leaned over and pulled the handle, thrusting open the bus door. Then he glanced back at me. "Last stop, kid. Everyone out." He laughed. The big, stupid hunk of meat laughed like that was the funniest joke in the world.

I got up. My whole body made little cracking sounds as I straightened out. My spine was having its own Fourth of July celebration, six months late. Thanks to all the construction on the highway, the ride here had taken two hours. That wasn't counting the half-hour trip to the city to meet the bus. Me and Dad. What fun that was. Dad didn't say a word when he handed me over to the driver. He just gave me that where-have-I-failed? look. I didn't say anything, either. I just gave him my how-would-I-know? look. He couldn't wait to get out of there.

"Come on, kid," the driver said. "I ain't got all day."

I grabbed my bag out of the overhead rack and scooped up my jacket from the seat. Mom would have made me wear the jacket. Probably a dorky scarf, too. But it wasn't all that cold for the beginning of January, and Mom wasn't around.

"Move it, kid."

I took my time strolling down the aisle.

"Have a nice life," the driver said as I walked past him. He laughed again, wheezing like a donkey with asthma.

"Have a heart attack," I said. Then I hopped to the ground before he could grab me.

Behind my back, I heard the door slam hard, cutting off the stream of swear words the driver was spewing at me. Some people sure are touchy.

I looked at the stiff little man with the bow tie.

"Hello, Martin," he said, smiling the sort of smile that doesn't mean anything. "I'm Principal Davis. Welcome to Edgeview."

I had no idea what he expected me to say. *Gee, nice place you have here, thanks for inviting me.* I waited. He didn't seem like the sort of person who would run out of words. I'm sure he had all sorts of wisdom to share with me. I hadn't met an adult yet who didn't have essential advice to pass along.

"Well, you have a bit of settling in to do. We'd better get started." He creaked his way up the steps toward the front door, muttering the basic facts of my life as if to prove he knew and cared. "Martin Anderson, age thirteen, grade eight, hometown is Spencer, recently expelled from Spencer Heights Middle School. Previously expelled from Upper Spencer Junior High, expelled before that from . . ."

I tuned him out. To my right, the bus rolled out through the gate and rumbled down the road, carrying the driver back to the free world. I followed Principal Davis inside the building. The entrance was dark, barely lit by two weak bulbs that hung from the ceiling on frayed cords. The air hung down over me, too. Warm and heavy air. I felt like I was breathing soup.

We climbed a steep flight of stairs to the left of the front door. The steps ended in the middle of a long hallway. Something that might have been a carpet a million footsteps ago clung to the floor. More dim bulbs made a halfhearted attempt at lighting the area, revealing walls covered with scrawled graffiti.

"I assume you understand why you are here," Principal Davis said.

"I got on the wrong bus?" I figured a very stupid question deserved an extremely stupid answer.

He ignored my guess and kept walking, leading me up a second flight of steps. The wall felt rough, and the dull green paint had flaked away in a couple of spots. The odor of old varnish on the second floor gave way to the sharper stench of unwashed clothing as I climbed higher.

I tried again. "I won a contest? I wrote the winning essay? I'm the tenth caller? I got the highest score in Final Jeopardy?" This was fun. And as long as I kept talking, I wouldn't have to think about where I was going.

"These are the living quarters," he said, still ignoring my guesses. "After you've gotten settled, I'll have someone give you a tour of the school." He stopped where he was and I caught up to him. Actually, I almost ran into him. His suit smelled like dusty mothballs.

"I know," I said as the perfect answer hit me. "I'm here because you need an assistant. The place is too much for you to handle by yourself. You just aren't up to the job."

Oops. That one got rid of his smile. His face turned mean and angry for an instant—the sort of meanness that needs to lash out and cause pain. I could almost hear his teeth grinding together. Unlike the smile, this was an honest expression. This was Principal Davis at his finest. If he'd been a cartoon character, steam would have shot from his nose and ears. But, like a true professional, he hid the anger quickly. "Well, now . . . no point standing here chattering. Let's get you—"

He never finished that sentence. From down the hall, we were interrupted by a shout: "FIRE!"

TELEPHONE CONVERSATION BETWEEN THE PARENTS OF MARTIN ANDERSON

Richard Anderson: Hi. It's me. I got the kid to the bus. I stopped at the office on the way home.

Dorothy Anderson: Do you think he'll be okay?

Richard Anderson: Who knows? I hope this place does him some good. Heaven knows nothing else has worked. I'll tell you, my old man wouldn't have let me get away with anything. He'd have smacked me a couple of good ones with his belt. That always kept me in line. I don't know where the kid gets that mouth of his.

Dorothy Anderson: Martin's not that bad.

Richard Anderson: Tell that to the last three schools he's been kicked out of. Tell that to the scout troop that threw him out. And while you're at it, try telling it to his Little League coach. You know how bad that made me look when he mouthed off to the coach?

Dorothy Anderson: It's my fault. I just know it. I saw this psychologist on a talk show, and he said—

Richard Anderson: Forget that nonsense. And don't blame yourself. Or me. It's not our fault. It's his fault. We're good parents. His sister is turning out fine. We did everything we could. Listen, want me to pick up a pizza on the way home?

Dorothy Anderson: I guess. Yeah, that would be nice.

FLAMING OUT

When I heard the kid shout, "FIRE!" my brain said, *Get out of here*, but my feet said, *Freeze*.

My feet won.

Suddenly, kids were running all over the place. Along both sides of the hall, doors flew open and kids popped out, almost like they were throwing a giant surprise party. Far down at the end of the hall, smoke drifted from a room. There wasn't a lot of smoke—just a trickle—but any smoke is bad if it isn't supposed to be there. At least the fire wasn't between me and the stairs. I relaxed when I realized I wasn't trapped.

"It's Torchie's room," one kid said. "He did it again."

Principal Davis sighed. "I told them to make sure he didn't get any matches," he said. "Can't anyone around here carry out a simple order? Do I have to do everything myself?"

"Coming through," someone shouted from behind us.

A guy raced up the stairs carrying a fire extinguisher. He sprinted past us and hurried toward the room. I followed, trying to slip my way through the crowd that had gathered at the edge of the smoke. I managed to squeeze next to the doorway and catch a glimpse inside the room. A small fire smoldered on a desk. It looked like a bunch of papers were burning. A kid stood pressed against the far wall, staring at the fire. I figured that must be Torchie.

"I didn't do it," he said. "Honest, I didn't do nuthin'." He raised his hands in a display of innocence. A trickle of sweat ran down his forehead, past his right eye. It stopped, finally, at his pudgy cheek. Red hair, also damp, drooped in clumps from a wandering part that ran along the center of his scalp. It was the sort of face a ventriloquist would have loved. "I didn't do it," he repeated.

Yeah, right, I thought. *And I'm Abe Lincoln.* In the room, the guy with the fire extinguisher let fly with a stream of foamy spray, knocking out the blaze pretty quickly. He spun toward the crowd of kids and spouted out words I never would have expected. "Quick, what have we learned here?"

Nobody said anything. I sure didn't.

"Come on," the man said. "This is easy. What three things are required for a fire?"

"Heat, fuel . . . " a small kid at the back of the crowd said. I couldn't believe the guy was turning this into a science lesson. He had to be a teacher, though he sure wasn't dressed like one. He wore a T-shirt with PRINCETON on it in big orange letters hanging above a picture of a tiger. The shirt was tucked into a pair of jeans. The frayed jeans cuffs hung over scuffed shoes, the same way his ragged mustache hung over his upper lip.

"Right! Heat and fuel. That's two. Come on, one more," the man urged. He took a real deep breath.

"Oxygen," someone else said.

"Exactly!" The guy held up the extinguisher. "So we smother the fire to deprive it of oxygen. We can also stop a fire by lowering the temperature or removing the fuel. Remember that." He gave the desktop another short blast. Then he turned his attention to Torchie. I wondered if he was going to blast the kid with a stream of words the way he'd blasted the fire with a stream of foam, but he just sighed and said, "Philip, we need to work a bit harder on this problem of yours." He tucked the extinguisher under his left arm and held his right hand out, palm up.

Torchie—I guess his real name was Philip—opened his mouth as if he was going to protest. Then he shrugged, reached into his pants pocket, and pulled out a disposable lighter. "I really didn't do nuthin'," he said as he dropped the lighter in the man's hand. "Honest."

What a loser.

The man didn't say anything more to Torchie. He put the lighter in his own pocket, then turned back to the crowd and said, "Okay, guys, it's all over. Nothing else to see. Move along." He sounded like a city cop trying to get people away from an accident, but I sort of liked that.

"Well," Principal Davis said, coming up behind me, "this works out rather nicely. Now that you're together, allow me to introduce you to your roommate. Martin Anderson, meet Philip Grieg."

My roommate? Oh crap. This had to be a joke.

Torchie looked at the principal and spewed out the double-negative denial yet again. "I didn't do nuthin'." His eyes shifted over toward me as if he hoped I could leap to his defense. *Keep dreaming, fireboy.*

"We'll deal with that issue later, Philip. For now, why don't you be a good lad and show Martin around the school. I have to get back to my office."

With that, Principal Davis marched off, leaving me alone in the company of Philip or Torchie or whatever his flaming name was. I stared after the principal. That was it? Hi. Bye. Rip me from my home and shove me here. I had no choice except to turn back to my new roommate.

Now that it was just the two of us, I figured Torchie would find a different song. No such luck. "I really didn't do it," he said.

Sheesh—he needed a sign with that printed on it. Or one of those big pin-on buttons. Then he could just point whenever he wanted to claim he was innocent. I waited for him to change the subject. He wiped his face with his sleeve. It didn't do much for his face, and it left a big wet blotch on his shirt.

"Didn't do nuthin'," he said.

"So I heard." This was just great. They'd put me in a room with a kid who liked to start fires. Fantastic. If I'd known ahead of time, I'd at least have brought some marshmallows. We could have toasted them. Hot dogs would be nice, too. As it was, I hoped I didn't end up getting toasted myself. Man, we'd be a great pair if that happened. Torchie and Toastie.

I glanced at the window to make sure it was big enough for me to squeeze through in an emergency. As far as I could see, there wasn't a fire escape. At least there weren't any bars. On the other hand, this was the third floor, so I hoped I'd never have to use the window as an exit.

One of the two beds in the room was under the window. From the rumpled look, and a couple of burn marks on the sheets, I figured it was Torchie's. The other bed, along the opposite wall, was unmade, but a pile of sheets and blankets were stacked on it, along with a photocopied booklet that said *Welcome to Edgeview* on the cover. I took a quick glance through the booklet, saw nothing important, then tossed it into the small garbage can next to the bed. There wasn't much else in the room, just two old wooden desks, two small dressers, also made of wood, a pair of lamps, and a closet. A picture of Mars, torn from a magazine, was taped to one wall near the foot of Torchie's bed. Great. Except for the lamps and garbage can, everything in the room looked flammable. To top it off, the place already smelled like the inside of a fireplace. I tossed my bag to the floor by the closet.

"What are you here for?" Torchie asked.

"What do you care?" I asked back.

He shrugged. "I don't know. Just wondering. Figured, being roommates and all, I should get to know you. And maybe you'd want to know about me. Some of the people here aren't too friendly. Not me. I like people."

I held up my hand to shut him off. "I'm here because I seem to have a bit of a problem respecting authority. That's how they put it. Well, that's how the polite ones put it. I've also been called a major pain in the butt, a disturbing influence, a smart mouth, and a snotty-nosed little puke, among other things." I didn't bother adding some of Dad's more colorful phrases. There was no point telling this fire freak my life's story. Not that he'd care.

I stared at the charred pieces of papers scattered around the desk and the bits of extinguisher foam dripping slowly onto the rug. What a mess. It looked like a giant cow had let loose with one monster of a sneeze. "And you're here because you have a hard time with math, right?"

"Huh?" Poor Torchie seemed a bit puzzled.

"Just kidding." I could see this was going to be a lot of fun. I reached down toward my bag. But I didn't want to unpack yet. That would make it real. "So, you feel like showing me around? Principal Davis didn't exactly give me a detailed introduction to the place."

"Yeah. Sure." Torchie led me into the hall and started giving me the tour of Edgeview Alternative School.

**MEMO PAD
ON PRINCIPAL
DAVIS'S DESK**

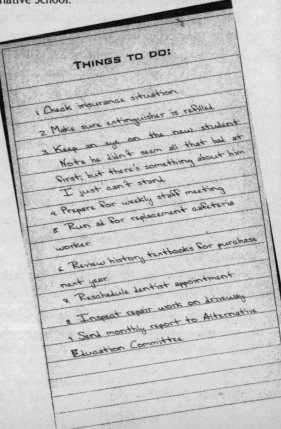

THINGS TO DO:

1 Check insurance situation.

2 Make sure extinguisher is refilled

3 Keep an eye on the new student
Note he didn't seem all that bad at
first, but there's something about him
I just can't stand

4 Prepare for weekly staff meeting

5 Run ad for replacement cafeteria
worker.

6 Review history textbooks for purchase
next year.

7 Reschedule dentist appointment.

8 Inspect repair work on driveway

9 Send monthly report to Alternative
Education Committee

How about a unit on using science facts in everyday life? I think the kids would like that. Everyday occurrences like a dormitory fire or a small explosion present a wonderful opportunity for a lesson. What else? Maybe I could do something with food. That's always popular.

TAKING THE TOUR

*L*ip and Bloodbath live in that room," Torchie told me, pointing to a door near the stairs. "Lip's no problem by himself. Heck, he's almost a midget. But Bloodbath likes to beat on people. He's in our grade, but he's almost sixteen. Keep out of his way."

"Thanks." This was useful information. It was nice knowing where the toilets were and stuff like that, but I was a lot more interested in learning who could hurt me. "Why do they call him *Bloodbath*?"

"That's his last name."

"You're kidding."

"Nope," Torchie said. His voice dropped to a whisper. "He's Lester Bloodbath."

"Anyone call him Lester?" I asked.

"Nobody who's still alive." Torchie shrugged, then led me around the rest of the hall, telling me who was in most of the rooms. There were a lot of nicknames, none of which I'd be proud to own. One kid was called Goober Gobble, for reasons I wouldn't want to think about on an empty stomach. And there was the unfortunate Patrick Pardeau, who had to go through every day of his life being greeted with his initials. "Hi, PeePee."

"That's Waylon," Torchie whispered, pointing to a small kid who was walking down the hall away from us. "But we call him Hindenburg."

"Why?" I asked.

Torchie grinned. "You know what the Hindenburg was?"

"An airship. Like a blimp, except it's rigid," I said, remembering a picture I'd seen. "It's a bag full of gas."

"Yup," Torchie said. "And so's Waylon."

"That little guy?"

Torchie nodded. "He's deadly. Don't ever get in a small space near him. Especially when they serve cabbage or beans at lunch." He stuck out his tongue and made a farting sound.

Call me weak—I laughed. I also felt relieved. With Hindenburg labeled as the school's gas man, there's no way I'd get stuck with a nickname like *Fartin' Martin*. Not that I had any problem in that area, but the easy rhyme made that sort of thing a danger.

Torchie introduced me to several kids, but my brain was already getting overloaded with names and faces, so none of it really stuck right away. I'd guess most of them didn't remember my name, either. Not that I'd expect them to. All in all, it was kind of a relief actually meeting some of the students. I'd figured I was getting dumped on an island filled with nothing but ax murderers and cannibals. So far, I hadn't seen either. Just seventh, eighth, and ninth graders.

"What are the classes like?" I asked as we headed down from the dorm rooms to the second floor.

"Depends," Torchie said. "Some of the teachers are big-time strict. I think one or two of them should be locked up somewhere themselves. Miss Nomad is nice. She's the English teacher. Once we get her talking, she'll chatter for the whole period, so we really don't have to do much work. Just say *Shakespeare* and she's good for an hour. Mr. Briggs, the science teacher, is pretty cool. He's the one who came in with the fire extinguisher."

I didn't care about the teachers right now. I wanted to find out more about discipline, since I seemed to get a major dose of it wherever I went. "So, are you in trouble for that fire?"

Torchie nodded. I noticed that some of his hair was singed at the tips. "Yup, I'm in trouble," he said.

"What'll they do to you?"

He shook his head. "That's the scary part. You never know what they'll think up. They keep trying different stuff on us. It's like we're some kind of rats in a lab. Honest. They try something different every time."

"Does it work?" As I asked him that, I realized it was a stupid question. If the punishment had worked, Torchie wouldn't have been barbecuing papers in his room.

He spread his arms out in a gesture of total innocence. "How can it work? I didn't do nuthin'. They keep trying to cure me, but I didn't start the fire. That lighter was empty. Just like these." He reached into his right pocket and pulled out a handful of disposable lighters. He flicked one a couple of times, throwing a shower of sparks. "See? No flames. I just like the sparks."

Oh boy. I could tell there was no point trying to get Torchie to face reality. I'd known kids like that before. You could stand there and watch them do something—hit another kid, break a window, steal from a store. And then, if you accused them, they'd look right at you and say, "I didn't do it." I'd known all kinds of liars. Some enjoyed it. Some couldn't help it. And a few poor losers didn't even know they were lying.

But that was his problem. I wanted more details about what might happen to me. I imagined dozens of kids locked in dungeons, dangling from chains while a huge, sweaty guy wearing a leather apron heated up torture tools. The image made me shudder and laugh at the same time. I could just picture what would happen if they went near Hindenburg with a red-hot poker. Kaboom. Lots of little Hinden-bits flying through the air. "What sort of stuff do they try for punishment?" I asked. "They ever hit you?"

Torchie shook his head. "Not too much. They might take away privileges, or make you watch some stupid old video on how to behave, or force you to listen to a lecture. You'll find out."

"Guess I will. Come on, show me the rest of the place."

I followed Torchie down to the second floor. He pointed to one room at the end of the hall. "Teachers take turns staying there overnight and on weekends. I don't know why they bother having someone else around, since Principal Davis almost never goes home. Past that side of the stairs is more dorm rooms. The rest of the floor is classrooms." He opened a couple of the doors so I could see for myself.

The classrooms were pretty much the same as any other classrooms I'd ever been in. Poorly erased blackboards and uneven rows of chairs and desks left no mistake what went on during the week. Most of the stuff didn't match. I noticed at least three different kinds of desks in the first room, and lots of different chairs. I guess even the furniture was stuff nobody else wanted. Edgeview seemed to be a final rest stop on the way to the scrap yard. One classroom didn't have any desks or chairs. All I saw was a rug spread out on the floor.

"That's Mr. Briggs's room," Torchie said as we looked in. "He brought the rug himself. He keeps experimenting with different learning environments. It's a good place to catch a nap."

I was about to turn around when I got this feeling someone was staring at the back of my neck. Then I turned around and found that the feeling was a fact. For an instant, I thought I was about to meet a teacher. That's how big the guy behind me was. When reality sunk in, I checked the hall for a quick escape route.

"I'm Bloodbath," the guy said, stepping close enough to cut off any hope I had of sprinting away. He looked about half the size of the bus driver, which was still a lot bigger than any kid had a right to be. No fat—all the weight was muscle. The way Torchie had talked about him, I expected him to be some kind of troll. But he could have passed for one of those actors who makes a couple of movies, gets real popular with the girls for a year or two, and then vanishes from sight. He had that kind of face.

He wasn't alone. There was another kid with him. He barely came up to my shoulders. I was pretty sure, based on Torchie's description, that the other kid was Lip. Lip was so ugly I had a hard time taking my eyes from his face—it was like staring at a traffic accident.

Bloodbath glanced over at Torchie, then tilted his head slightly. He didn't say a word. But Torchie got the message. He swallowed, blinked a couple of times like a puzzled turtle, and took off. He started out walking, but broke into a jog as soon as he got a few steps away. I had the impression he couldn't wait to leave. What a pal. Yup—we roommates sure stick together.

Bloodbath turned his attention back to me. "Welcome to Edgeview," he said, putting a large hand on the doorframe next to my shoulder. A small silver ring dangled from his left nostril. I had this crazy urge to reach out and yank the ring off, but I knew if I did, it would be my last act on planet Earth.

I waited, figuring that, just like Principal Davis, Bloodbath had plenty more to talk about.

"Ding dong," Bloodbath said. "You hear that? That's the school bell."

As he said *school bell*, he gave me a shove, pushing me into the empty classroom. "And guess what?" he added as the two of them followed me in and closed the door. "It's time for your first lesson."

NOTE RECENTLY ADDED TO
LESTER BLOODBATH'S PERMANENT FILE

Lester is obviously troubled, but he does seem to display some wonderful leadership qualities. It's quite apparent that others admire him. They definitely take notice when he enters a room. We must encourage him to develop these qualities.

BloodbathRULES!!!!!

Kill

Hate is grate

This place sucks

Lets break some bones

The top of Lester Bloodbath's desk

TEACHING WITHOUT A LICENSE

I thought of a million things to say. The problem was that out of those million things, there were probably at least nine hundred thousand that would instantly get me on Bloodbath's bad side. Chances are, he didn't even have a good side. He seemed like the sort of kid who'd hurt his friends as quickly as he'd hurt anyone else. I figured the best thing to do was to let him think I was a spineless wimp who'd stand there and take whatever he did to me.

"Lesson one," Bloodbath said, moving very close to me. "This is my school. The teachers might think they run it, but I'm in charge. Got it?"

"You're in charge," I said. As ridiculous at that sounded, the parrot routine seemed the safest way to go. It took a lot of effort to keep my voice from sounding like I was mocking him. But so far he hadn't knocked my head off, so I guess I was doing okay. He reminded me of those explosives that blow up if you touch them the wrong way. Sometimes they even blow up without being touched.

"Two, anything you get, you share with me. You get a package from home, you share with me." He moved even closer, pressing his chest against mine. I tried not to gag as his breath washed over me. "Understand?"

"No problem," I said. "You can have everything I get from my folks." That was a painless promise. I wasn't expecting anything. Mom might have a moment of weakness and think about mailing me a box of cookies or something, but Dad wouldn't let her do that. *You don't reward bad behavior*, he'd say to her.

Bloodbath was so close now, I could count the hairs in his eyebrows. "Three, you tell anyone about this and I'll kill you. Got it?"

I nodded. I didn't trust myself to open my mouth. One wrong word and he'd kick the crap out of me. And if there was anything I had a talent for, it was saying the wrong word. Lots of wrong words. The craziest thing is that, as tense as I felt, part of me wanted to laugh in his face.

Bloodbath smiled. "Good. Now, just to make sure you understand my rules, here's a little something to help you remember." He stepped back and nodded at the other kid.

"Yeah," the kid said. His voice reminded me of someone who'd sucked a lungful of helium out of a balloon. He grinned, giving me a view of stained teeth jutting like a fifty-year-old picket fence from his rotting gums. "Here's a little something to help you remember." He punched me in the stomach.

My first thought was, *Huh?* I glanced down at his fist, which was still flat against my shirt, barely depressing the fabric. The kid had the weakest punch I'd ever felt. He'd hit me with about as much power as someone would use to burp a baby. My second thought was that it might be smart if I pretended he'd hurt me. Then they'd leave me alone. But that thought came a couple of seconds too late. If I dropped down now, I'd look as phony as one of those professional wrestlers who spends about five minutes reacting to a kick in the face.

"Lip, how many times have I told you?" Bloodbath asked. He reached out, grabbed Lip's shoulder, and yanked him aside. "You've got to put your body into it. Your whole body. And turn your shoulder. Like this."

Bloodbath lashed out and hit me in the stomach. As his fist shot into my gut and drove all the air out of my body, I bent over, then crumpled to the floor. For an instant, I didn't feel anything other than a huge numbness. That didn't last. Moments later, the pain flared out like an explosion. I curled up, waiting for the hurt to go away and wondering if I'd ever be able to breathe again.

I could dimly hear Lip through the waves of pain, saying, "Yeah, I get it. Kind of like swinging a bat."

I curled up tighter, hoping that Bloodbath wasn't going to start throwing kicks into my ribs or let Lip practice his punches on me. But it sounded like they were leaving.

"Catch you later, pal," Bloodbath said, walking out of the room and closing the door. I glanced over to make sure he'd left. A second later, he stuck his head back in. "Oh, don't forget to shut the lights off when you leave."

I turned my head away and closed my eyes. Even as I lay there, fighting the urge to throw up a breakfast I barely remembered eating, I thought about how I was going to get back at him. This was not the end of it. One way or another, Bloodbath would pay for hurting me. It might take a while, but I didn't think either of us was going anywhere in the near future. I'd have plenty of time to get even.

The door opened again. I heard muffled footsteps. "Don't feel bad," Torchie said. "He greets all the new kids that way."

I tried to answer, but I still couldn't catch my breath. So I lay there with my face in the rug. At least it was a nice rug—very deep and plush.

"Hey, cheer up," Torchie told me. "He'll probably leave you alone for a while. He gets bored pretty easily. Come on, let me give you a hand."

Torchie grabbed my arm and pulled. I managed to get to my knees. The pain was just a dull ache now—no worse than if a car had rolled over my stomach. I signaled for him to stop, then took several deep breaths. I felt like I was trying to force air into a hot water bottle. Finally, I got to my feet.

"So, want to see any more of the school?" Torchie asked. "The cafeteria and the gym are on the first floor."

"No. I've seen enough. Thanks." The effort to talk cost me more than I was willing to give at the moment.

I followed him upstairs toward the room. Our room. There were a lot more people in the halls than before. I figured they were checking me out. Almost all of the kids we passed stared at me, probably trying to guess how badly Bloodbath had hurt me. Word spreads faster than fire in a place like this. And most of the students had probably been through the same little ritual with Bloodbath. I had to show them I was tough. I stood up straight and managed to walk to the room without grabbing my stomach or groaning.

"You got a nickname?" Torchie asked after I'd collapsed on my bed.

"Nope."

"Lots of the kids here have them."

"I've noticed." It didn't hurt as much, but I still wasn't eager to talk.

The conversation went on like that for a while, with Torchie carrying almost all of it. He kept talking as he got to work cleaning up the soggy mess of fire-extinguisher foam and charred paper on top of his desk. In the next half hour, I learned where he was from (Newlins Falls), where his parents were from (Irish and Scottish on his mom's side, Swedish with a dash of French Canadian on his dad's side), what he liked to eat (burgers, lasagna, grilled cheese sandwiches), and full biographies of his last seven pets—three fish, two hamsters, a bird, and a lizard named Scooter.

After a while, I rolled off the bed and started unpacking my clothes. At least I didn't have to worry about how I looked. From what I'd seen so far, I wouldn't stand out like some kind of clueless loser. When I was done, I kicked my empty bag into the corner of the room. It felt so good, I kicked it again. Naturally, I pretended the bag was the crumpled body of Lester Bloodbath.

Torchie glanced up from the comic book he was reading. "It's not that bad here—honest."

How could he say that? Until today—until this morning—I'd lived at home. Now I lived here. How in the world could it not be bad? It looked like it was time to tell Torchie exactly what I thought about him and this whole stinking place.

CRUMPLED LETTER IN THE WASTEBASKET OF DOROTHY ANDERSON

Dear Martin,

How are you? I guess that's a stupid question. I didn't want you to go, but there was no choice. At least, no choice your father would accept. Even if we found another school near here, there'd still be problems. I wish I understood. Maybe someday I will.

I know you've been gone for less than a day, but I miss you. So I just wanted to write and let you know that I'm thinking about you.

Love,
Mom

FROM STATE SENATE BILL SJ-35A

School districts in each of the specified multi-county regions are authorized to establish an alternative school for the education of at-risk students, including those students who have been expelled from public schools for reasons including, though not limited to, violence, weapons violations, and disruptive behavior.

Each alternative school will be subject to evaluation during its fifth year of operation. At the termination of the evaluation period, the Alternative Education Committee will report its findings to the state Board of Education, along with recommendations for continuance, replacement, or dismantling of the program.

WHAT'S SHORT AND SMART
AND FUN TO TEASE?

I was interrupted by a knock on the door. A short kid wearing glasses with thick black frames stuck his head in. "I brought back your magazine," he said to Torchie.

"Come on in," Torchie said.

The kid walked in and handed a car magazine to Torchie. He turned to me and said, "Hi."

"That's Dennis Woo," Torchie said. "But everyone calls him Cheater."

Cheater glared at Torchie. "Not everyone. And it's a lie. I never cheat. I don't have to." He turned back toward me. "Let me ask you this. Do I look like someone who needs to cheat on tests?" He stood very still, as if that would help me see what a wise and honest person he was.

"No, you look awfully smart," I told him. "Heck, you look so smart I'd probably try to copy off of your tests. Maybe I can sit next to you in class."

He grinned. "Hey, thanks. You're okay."

I shrugged. Apparently, the subtle art of sarcasm was wasted on him. I glanced over at Torchie, trying not to grin. But I couldn't help rolling my eyes toward the ceiling.

"Wait, I get it," Cheater said. "You're playing with me, aren't you? You think I didn't know what you meant."

"Relax. I was just kidding." I didn't feel like making any more enemies—even little ones with thick glasses. I held out my hand. "No hard feelings?"

Cheater looked at me for a moment, as if trying to decide whether I was going to play some kind of joke on him. Then he reached out to shake hands. As he did, I suddenly wondered whether he was going to flip me through the air.

I guess my expression changed enough that he could figure out what was on my mind. "Relax," he said. "You look like you think I'm going to kung fu you or something. Talk about stereotypes. Just because I'm Chinese, you think I'm some kind of karate kid. Let me tell you, I don't know any of that stuff. I wish I did."

We shook hands. "I really was just kidding," I told him.

"Hey, I'm used to it," Cheater said. "My ancestors have been kicked around for centuries. But you know what? I don't think people hate us because we look different. I think they hate us because we're smart. I have a cousin who gets beaten up at least once a week because he always gets one hundred on his tests. You see? That's why people hate us."

Wow, I didn't want to get any deeper into that discussion. If someone hated you, did it really matter why? I didn't know. Maybe it mattered. At least there didn't seem to be any prejudice about who went to Edgeview. From what I'd seen, the place was about as mixed as any school I'd ever been to. Trouble was color-blind.

"I really do know lots of stuff," Cheater said. "Ask me anything. Did you know karate started out in China? Then it went to Okinawa in the sixteen hundreds. Didn't get to Japan until 1910. Edgeview Alternative School was built in 1932. But it started out as a factory. They rebuilt it twenty years ago. But it's just been a school for the last four and a half years."

"He really does know just about everything," Torchie said. "It's kind of amazing."

"Come on, ask me anything," Cheater said.

I realized he wasn't going to stop until I asked him a question. "Who invented radium?"

"Marie Curie. With her husband Pierre. In 1898. For which they got the Nobel Prize in 1903." He stared at me as if I'd just asked him to spell *cat*. "Come on. Torchie could have answered that one."

"Hey," Torchie said.

"Sorry," Cheater told him. He looked back at me.

All right. I'd give him my hardest question. "Who played the monster in *Abbot and Costello Meet Frankenstein*?" That was a real stumper. Most people would guess Boris Karloff. They'd be wrong.

Cheater didn't even blink. "Glenn Strange," he said, giving the correct answer.

Wow. I guess he really might know everything. Except how to stay out of trouble.

A bell rang in the hall.

"Dinnertime," Torchie announced, getting to his feet like someone who had just been invited to take a stroll to the electric chair.

"I'll grab some seats," Cheater said, dashing out the door.

"They short on seats?" I asked Torchie.

He shook his head. "No. Cheater just likes to be first in line." Then he leaned over to whisper, even though we were alone. "He doesn't really need glasses. But he kept bugging his folks for them. Don't tell him I told you. Okay?"

"Sure." I followed Torchie out the door. "How's the food?" I asked as we walked toward the stairs. I noticed that nobody seemed to be in a rush. I scanned the halls for Bloodbath and spotted him safely ahead of us.

"On a good day, it stinks," Torchie said. "But you'll get used to it."

We joined the herd shuffling toward the cafeteria on the first floor. Even from far off, as the smells reached me I got the feeling Torchie wasn't kidding about the food. I grabbed a tray and went through the line with Torchie, letting a bored-looking woman with a net over her hair and clear plastic gloves on her hands give me a plate loaded with various piles of glop. I wondered if the gloves were for our protection or for hers.

We wove our way between the round tables that seemed to have been dropped at random on the cracked linoleum floor, heading toward Cheater, who stood there signaling his success in getting some seats by waving one arm. As I followed Torchie to our spot near the far wall and plunked down on a wobbly plastic chair, I could see that the kids were split up into different groups, with anywhere from four to eight kids at a table. I'd guess there were about two hundred kids altogether. Bloodbath was hanging out with a bunch of tough guys at a couple tables in one corner. Everything about them—clothes, hair, attitude—said, *Don't mess with us*. The tables nearest them were empty. I guess nobody wanted to get too close to the sharks.

On a hunch, I looked at the table farthest from Bloodbath. Yup, the smallest, most scared kids were all clustered there, like a bunch of little bait fish.

"We used to have more tables," Torchie said. "But they got rid of all the square ones last month." He almost had to shout. There was a lot more talking than eating going on around us, filling the room with noise that seemed to wash over me from every direction.

"Rectangles," Cheater said, correcting him. "They were longer than they were wide. So that made them—"

"Yeah, whatever," Torchie said, glaring at Cheater. "Anyhow, I guess they figured round tables would make us behave better or something."

"Fascinating." I turned my attention to choking down the food. It's hard to believe that anyone could ruin macaroni and cheese, but the school cooks had managed to do just that. And the potatoes were awful. "These mashed potatoes really suck," I said.

"That's because they're turnips," Cheater explained. "A popular food source in Germany before the introduction of the potato."

I decided not to ask what the stringy green stuff was. Until now, I'd thought Mom was a pretty bad cook. Her idea of tomato sauce was ketchup with a dash of parmesan cheese. As I ate, I realized she could have been far worse. And at least back home we'd have takeout chicken once a week from Cluck Shack, and lots of pizza. I guess I wouldn't be getting anything like that for a while.

Between bites, I checked out my companions. Besides Torchie and Cheater, there was one other kid at our table. He looked pretty tough. Big shoulders, dark hair, eyebrows that seemed to want to grow together to form one furry strip across his forehead, and the beginnings of a stubbly beard threatening to burst through his skin. A year or two from now, I'd bet he'd be shaving twice a day. They called him Lucky. I almost laughed when I heard that. I didn't see how anyone who deserved that nickname could be stuck in a place like Edgeview. *Unlucky* was more like it. Or maybe *Unfriendly*. He didn't seem all that happy to meet me.

Not that I cared.

By the time I'd choked down half the macaroni, I had the whole place figured out. Except for one person.

Dear Mom and Dad,

I got a new roommate. He's cool. We get along great. I've been showing him around. He seemed kinda scared at first, but I guess that's normal. He looks kinda like Cousin Walter. You know. Brown hair and blue eyes. But his nose is smaller. Well, I guess everyone's nose is smaller than Walter's. And he has both ears. Oh yeah, his name's Martin.

I'm working real hard and learning lots of stuff. Mr. Parsons said my last report was almost intelligible. That's exactly what he wrote. I guess that's good. And Miss Nomad told me I had a flare for spontaneous expression. That's exactly what she wrote, too. Whatever that means.

I'm still really sorry about the parrot. Even though I didn't do it. Honest. I'm sure the feathers will grow back.

Well, I guess that's it for now.

Your son,
Philip

BREAK TIME

I'd watched him on and off during the meal, and I didn't have a clue why he was by himself. Well, as my dad always said, if you don't know the answer, ask a question. Of course, whenever I asked *him* a question, he usually told me to shut up and stop being such a wise ass.

But dad wasn't here, so I figured it was safe to ask a question.

"Who's the loner?" I asked Torchie, looking over toward the kid eating all by himself at a table near the opposite wall. There was nothing I could see about his clothes or appearance that would explain his isolation.

"Him? That's Trash."

"Nice name," I said.

"It's not like that. It's just that he trashes stuff. You know, breaks things."

"Yeah," Cheater said. "I heard that at his last school, he smashed up a whole classroom—desks, chairs, windows. The kid's wacko."

I looked back at Trash. It was hard to imagine why someone would break stuff for fun.

"Hey," Lucky said to Cheater, "you shouldn't say *wacko*. It's not nice."

"Yeah, you're right," Cheater said. "My mistake. He's not wacko—he's bonkers. Or maybe he's loony. How about *deranged*? I like that one."

"How'd you like to be called that?" Lucky asked.

"I think I'd prefer *insane*, if you're going for technical terms," Cheater said. "But *flipped out* has a nice ring to it. And let's not forget all those wonderful phrases that can be used to indicate a mind that is somewhat less than perfect: one card short of a full deck, one sandwich short of a picnic, off your rocker, out in left field—the list goes on and on. Hey, do you know where the word *bedlam* comes from? It was a crazy house in England."

"Listen," Lucky told him, his voice dropping so low I had to lean forward to catch the rest of it. "If enough people call you crazy, maybe you begin to believe it, even if you aren't."

All three of them started arguing about putting labels on people and about stuff like self-esteem. Everyone was talking at once. They sounded like a bunch of miniature psychiatrists. I guess they'd gotten a lot of that in class here. Personally, I thought they were all a bit crazy. Or wacko. Or bonkers. But I kept my mouth shut. I couldn't do much about kids like Bloodbath who'd hate me because that was how they treated everyone, but I didn't want to turn the whole place against me. I didn't want to end up eating dinner all by myself every day, like that pathetic loser they called Trash.

So I stayed quiet and let them go at it. Eventually, the argument faded out and everyone went back to eating.

"Well," Cheater said as we finished our meal, "welcome to Edgeview."

I was about to say, *Thanks*, when a crash from across the room made me jump. Nobody else seemed surprised. I realized Trash had thrown his plate down. It sounded like it had hit hard. I expected to see shattered pieces all over the floor, but the plate hadn't broken.

"He does that a lot," Torchie said. "They give him a plastic plate, so at least it doesn't break."

I watched Trash to see what he would do next. I wondered if he'd throw his fork, or maybe even his chair. Even though he was off on the other side of the room, I got ready to duck. But he just sat there. I couldn't see his face really well—he was hunched over and his hair hung down kind of long on the sides—but he didn't seem angry. He didn't seem happy, either. He actually appeared kind of sad.

"Wacko," Cheater said.

Lucky glared at him.

"What do you guys do after dinner?" I asked as we got up from the table.

"There's a TV in the lounge," Torchie said. "But Bloodbath and his gang hang out there."

"The library's not bad," Cheater added. "And on Friday nights, we all—"

"Play checkers," Lucky said.

He cut off Cheater so quickly I was sure they were hiding something. That was okay. I couldn't get angry over a secret or two. They didn't know me yet and they had no way to tell whether they could trust me. Just like I didn't really know yet if I could trust them.

"Yeah," Cheater said. "That's what I was going to say. We play checkers. Yup. Every Friday. That's what we do."

A bell rang, signaling the end of dinner. "Oh crap," I said as it hit me.

"What?" Torchie asked.

"Nothing." It wasn't a thought I felt like sharing, but I'd just realized my whole life was going to be measured by bells.

When we got back to the room, I borrowed a magazine from Torchie. He had a great selection—monster stuff, sports, comics, cars—though some of them looked like they'd been snatched from a fire. I read for a while, then decided to go to sleep. We had to turn out our lights at ten, anyhow, so it wasn't like I was missing anything.

Right about now, back home, I'd be saying good night to my sister.

Good night, you spoiled brat.

And she'd be saying good night to me.

Good night, you creepy little twerp.

It was sort of a ritual with us. Funny how, in one day, *home* had turned into *back home*. Somewhere else. Somewhere I wasn't.

I could hear Torchie across the room breathing. Out in the hall, it sounded like someone was wrestling. The walls shook with the thud of a body hitting hard. Maybe it was a fight. I didn't care. It had nothing to do with me.

Tomorrow was Monday. I'd get to find out firsthand what classes were like. Maybe these teachers would be better. Maybe I could get along with them.

I closed my eyes and thought about the places I'd been before Edgeview. All of a sudden, the other schools didn't seem that bad. Sure, there'd been a lot of jerks to deal with, but I guess there were jerks everywhere. Maybe I was a jerk myself for getting kicked out so often.

But this was it. Edgeview was the last place that would take me. This was the place for kids who had been thrown out of all the regular schools where they lived. Six counties in the northern part of the state had gotten together to make this dump. There was nowhere to go from here. Edgeview was my dead end.

THE THINKING HERO

DENNIS WOO

Magnus Cranium was the strongest man in the Legion of Ultra Heroes. He was also the smartest. Magnus could solve any problem with his incredible brain. One time, the super villain Rottenman trapped Magnus in a room made of titanium steel covered with an electric field and rigged with fifty atom bombs.

'No problem,' Magnus said. 'I can escape.'

Did he hit the walls? No. Did he push against the door? No. Magnus sat and thought. And the answer came to him. He saw a way out. It's too complicated to describe, because Magnus is so smart. It would be hard to understand, especially since it involved quantum mechanics and advanced particle physics. And maybe some karate. But he did it.

A LITTLE CLASS

A bell woke me.

"Good morning," Torchie called from across the room in a disgust-ingly cheerful voice.

I coughed a couple of times as I sat up, wondering why my lungs felt like I'd spent the night in an ashtray. The answer sat in the bottom of my wastebasket. I stared at the charred ball of burned paper that had once been a student handbook.

"Hey, are you trying to kill us?" I asked Torchie.

"I didn't do nothin'," he said.

"Right." There was no point arguing. We'd just get into one of those did-not, did-too things that don't go anywhere. So I dropped it and got ready for my day at Edgeview.

My first class after breakfast was math. When I reached the door, Cheater waved to me from the middle of the empty room. "I got us some seats," he said.

"Thanks." I plunked down next to him. "I was afraid I'd have to stand."

"I'm not going to copy off of you," Cheater added. "Everyone says I do. But I don't."

"Fine." I didn't care if he copied from me.

Torchie grabbed the seat on my other side. He'd sort of attached himself to me. That was okay—I didn't mind sticking with someone who knew what was going on. And, compared to a lot of the kids I'd seen, he was reasonably normal, if you didn't count his slight problem with fire. Besides, he was so relentlessly friendly that being mean to him would be like kicking a puppy. He didn't act like those kids who ask, *Will you be my friend?* Now, those kids I don't mind kicking. With Torchie, it was more like he was saying, *I'm going to be your friend.*

I didn't see any point fighting it.

Bloodbath wasn't in my math class, but I saw three kids just like him sitting in the back row. They all had that same deadly look. One had rings in his nose and in both eyebrows. He might have had a ring in his tongue, too, but I really didn't want to get close enough to see for sure. I didn't even want him to catch me looking in his direction. His buddy had a tattoo of a skull on his forehead. It looked like he'd done it himself. Just the thought of a needle being jabbed over and over into my flesh made me shudder. I wondered if his pea-sized brain realized the humor of putting a skull on the outside of his own skull. Probably not. The third beast in that cluster of thugs had GRUNGE tattooed on the back of each hand. As far as I could tell, none of them carried any books to class.

"Here comes Mr. Parsons," Torchie whispered as the teacher stepped into the room. "Careful. He's got a bit of a temper."

A teacher with a temper? Now, that was a shock. I watched Mr. Parsons walk to his desk. He looked pretty much like any of a million other middle-aged math teachers, except for the long strands of hair that he'd combed over the top of his head from the side. He was wearing a rumpled green jacket, rumpled green pants, and a blue tie—not a bow tie, but I still didn't trust him.

"Good morning, class," he said.

There was no answer, but about half of the kids at least glanced in his direction. One kid—I learned later that they called him Flying Dan—was running around at the back of the room with his arms spread out like airplane wings. Another was carving something on his desk with his pen. At least he was doing that until the pen snapped from the pres-

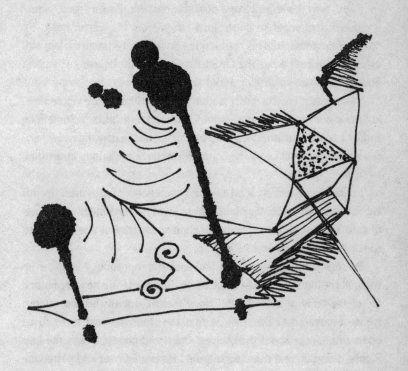

sure. A couple kids stared out the windows. And I guess I was looking all around the room at everyone else.

Mr. Parsons cleared his throat. I faced forward and tried to escape his notice. *Be cool*, I told myself. *Just sit back and get through it.* That was my plan.

"Well, now, I see we have a new student," Mr. Parsons said, glancing down at a sheet of paper he'd taken from his lesson book. He scanned the room until his eyes landed on me—not a tough trick to pull off, since I wasn't a moving target like Flying Dan. "Martin, why don't you tell the class something about yourself."

I shrugged. "There's really nothing to tell." I hated the whole new-kid song-and-dance routine—stand up, stutter a bit, say something totally stupid, sit down. What did he think I was, a dancing dog?

"Come on, don't be modest. Surely you have something interesting to share."

I shook my head. At least I wasn't the center of attention. In this class, there was no center of attention. I was just one bubble in a glass of cola, clinging to the side while a giant soda straw of a teacher tried to stir things around and suck us up.

Parsons shuffled over to me and smiled a thin smile. His upper lip was nearly the same pasty color as his forehead. The head reminded me of the belly of a dead fish. "Now, Martin, one of the basic things we've discovered at Edgeview is that the students must learn to be open and honest about themselves. Open and honest. That's the key. Please, stand up and share something." He leaned over and patted me on the shoulder, then returned to the front of the class and crossed his arms. His whole body said, *I'm waiting.*

It looked like there was no way out. I stared at him, standing straight ahead of me, acting all-powerful and filled with expert ideas and theories about what was right for us poor little students. Open and honest? As I rose to my feet, I realized that was the perfect description—I honestly had no idea what was going to come out when I opened my mouth.

"Hi. My name's Martin Anderson, and I'm not bald."

I sat back down.

Mr. Parsons's face grew red. Even the top of his scalp, through the strands of combed-over hair, turned the color usually only seen in ripe garden tomatoes. His face wasn't just changing color, it was also twitching, like in the monster movies right before a guy turns into a werewolf. I expected him to start shouting, but he whirled away from me, fumbled around for some chalk, and wrote the lesson on the board. He broke three pieces before he was finished.

I glanced over at Torchie. He held his finger up like a knife and ran it across his throat. Then he flopped his tongue out, closed his eyes, and dropped his head onto one shoulder. I guess that was his subtle way of telling me I'd probably not made a good first impression on Mr. Parsons.

"Way to go," Cheater whispered.

Yeah, way to go.

The class itself was pretty strange. I guess it was some kind of experimental teaching method. The idea seemed to be that we could learn math better if we didn't have to spend so much time memorizing stuff and just used numbers in lots of different ways.

I wasn't sure whether it would work, but I was willing to give it a try, and I certainly didn't want to get any further out on Mr. Parson's bad side—if that was possible—so I paid attention. I even raised my hand once or twice, though he didn't call on me.

Things didn't stay peaceful for long. About halfway through class, Mr. Parsons handed back some tests. When Cheater got his, he shouted, "It's not fair!" He jumped up, knocked over his desk, kicked his chair, and rushed from the room.

Nobody paid any attention. Not even the teacher. I glanced at the test where it had landed on the floor. On top, written in red pen, there was a large *F*. Then I looked over at Torchie.

"He'll be back," Torchie said.

Sure enough, Cheater returned a couple minutes later, acting as if nothing had happened. He put his desk back and sat down. The bell rang.

"Wow, you sure know how to blend in," Cheater said as we were leaving for our next class. He raced ahead.

"Yeah," Torchie said. "Parsons looked like he wanted to strangle you."

I shrugged. "He'll get over it. I didn't really say anything all that bad. I hope the other teachers aren't that sensitive. Is his class always like this?"

Torchie shook his head. "Parsons keeps trying different stuff. Last month, we had to learn a bunch of songs about fractions. There's this one jingle I still can't get out of my head."

"You're kidding."

He shook his head. "I wish I was."

Before I could ask him about our next class, someone punched me on the shoulder hard enough to knock me into the wall.

FORM 937-C EDGEVIEW SCHOOL

———————— FOR OFFICIAL USE ONLY ————————

NEW STUDENT PRELIMINARY EVALUATION FORM

Student Name: Martin Anderson

Evaluation: A vicious and destructive boy. That's my impression. He'll require close watching. I've met few students who are as unruly and ill mannered.

Evaluator: Mr. Luther Parsons

LETTER TO THE EDITOR

THE EDGEVIEW EXPRESS
DATED FIVE YEARS AGO

Dear Editor,
    I am firmly against the establishment of an alternative school in our town. We do not need problems like this. What will happen to our streets? Nobody will be safe. Edgeview should not be the dumping grounds for other people's problems.
                                    Mrs. Clarise V. Pitowski

A LITTLE MORE CLASS

*H*ey!" I shouted.

Bloodbath, passing by in the other direction, glanced back and grinned. I guess the punch was his way of saying hello. It would have been nice to return the greeting with a baseball bat, but there didn't seem to be one handy. I waited until he was out of sight before I rubbed the sore spot.

Torchie didn't even seem to notice. I guess punches from Bloodbath in the hallway were as common as mosquito bites near a swamp—a pain in the butt at times, but nothing unusual. Torchie stopped in front of an open door decorated with a picture of Shakespeare taped to the lower half. "Here we are. English class. You'll like Miss Nomad."

I followed Torchie inside, where we grabbed the seats Cheater had saved for us. Between them, I felt like I was sitting in a box full of puppies.

As the bell rang, Ms. Nomad swept into the room, her long skirt brushing the floor, her long brown hair brushing past her shoulders and flowing all the way to her waist. She wished us a cheery good morning, smiling as if today were the most wonderful day in the world and we were the most fabulous students a teacher could wish for. She was so young, I figured she couldn't have been teaching for more than a year or two. She zapped a huge grin in my direction and said, "Welcome to the class, Martin. Welcome, welcome, welcome. Feel free to join in the discussion." Oh man, she reminded me of some kind of life-size talking animal from a cartoon. She beamed an even bigger smile in my direction. It looked like she had more teeth than anyone would ever actually need.

I waited for her to say, *Tell us something about yourself.* I would have bet a million bucks she'd do that next. But she just picked up a book and started the lesson.

Perfect. I relaxed and sat back. Maybe we'd get along just fine. Everyone groaned when she pulled out a book of poetry, but I sort of liked the first part of the poem she read to us.

> Because I could not stop for death
> He kindly stopped for me.

I actually felt a chill when she read that. I didn't completely under-stand it, and I sure didn't understand the rest of the poem, but those two lines sounded pretty cool.

"I told you she was nice," Torchie whispered.

"Yeah." Maybe this class would be okay.

Unlike math, English class went well for almost ten minutes. At that point, we were talking about writing. "Writing is such a wonderful way to express yourself," Miss Nomad said. "And the best part is that *any-one* can write." She had a habit of walking all around the room as she talked, as if she were weaving herself among our desks. It made me feel like I was part of one of those pot holders kids make in craft classes. I was getting a sore neck from watching her. At the moment, she was passing right by me. As she said the word *anyone* she gave me this look that seemed to say, *Yes, Martin, even poor little you can scrawl meaningful words.* She almost seemed to expect a poem to burst from my forehead.

Move on, lady, I thought.

She stayed where she was, her smile burning a hole through my face. All that talk about only sharing when I felt like it—that was obviously a pile of crap. She wasn't going to budge until I spilled some warmth.

I raised my hand.

"Martin, you have something to contribute?" Miss Nomad asked. "That's wonderful. I'm so glad you've chosen to participate."

"Yeah. Maybe *anyone* can write, but won't some people stink at it? I mean, anyone can paint, but most people really stink at that. I know I do. The last painting I tried looked like dog puke. And the same for playing the violin or making a chair. Have you ever heard someone who's really bad on the violin? It's not very pleasant. And I sure wouldn't trust my butt sitting in any chair I'd made with these two hands."

She sort of gulped. In my mind, I saw this human goldfish that suddenly found herself stranded on dry land. Then the smile returned. "But that's the wonderful thing about writing. Nobody else can judge your work. As long as you think it's good, that's all that matters." She leaned over and stared at me with those big eyes, giving me that I-may-be-a-teacher-but-I-understand-you look. "Can't you see how wonderful a thing that is?" she asked.

Can't I see that you're a fruitcake?

I almost let it go, but I couldn't. She was wrong. I had an uncle who was always trying to write books. He'd send them out and they'd come back three or four months later with a printed slip that said, *No thanks.* Not even *Nice try*, or *Good effort*. Just *No thanks*. Which I think really meant: *Your book truly sucks. Please leave us alone.*

I tried to read some of his stuff once. It really stunk big-time. Talk about dog puke. Nothing ever happened. People just sat around and discussed life. Everyone drank coffee and felt bad about things they'd done in the past. I had a feeling Uncle Stan could write books for the next thousand years and he'd still stink. I looked up at Miss Nomad. She seemed so happy and eager for us to share the joys of writing.

"It matters," I said. "People might say they just write for themselves. That's a lie. Everyone wants to show off. And if you stink, you can't show off, can you? Because nobody will buy what you write. So you're just lying to yourself." I stopped talking. Damn. I didn't care either way. Why was I even bothering to say anything?

Miss Nomad gulped again, a bit louder, then said, "Well, thank you for sharing your thoughts, Martin."

I had the funny feeling she didn't like me.

"Bad move," Cheater whispered to me a minute later. "She's always trying to sell her poems. She keeps sending them to magazines."

"She's got hundreds of 'em," Torchie said. "Boxes full."

"And?" I asked.

"Hasn't sold a single one," Cheater told me. He shook his head. "Sometimes she reads them to us." He made a face and pinched his nose.

Yipes. I should have figured that out before I opened my big mouth. I could just imagine Miss Nomad, fountain pen in hand, sitting at a desk jammed in the corner of some small room, filling page after page with bad poetry. I didn't think she'd hold it against me the way Parsons did, but I'd certainly made sure I wouldn't be the teacher's pet in this class.

Miss Nomad pretty much ignored me for the rest of the period. I'd become the invisible boy. Hey, that could be a nickname for me—Glassboy. See right through me. I'm not really here.

When the bell rang, I checked my schedule. I had gym next. That would be more like it. Gym would be fun. Gym would be nice and normal—just run around and sweat. No matter how modern they got in their teaching methods, I didn't see how they could mess with something as simple as gym.

On the other hand, it's amazing what adults can do when they set their minds to it.

SAND

PRISCILLA NOMAD

A single grain of mighty sand,

I hold iT lovingly in my hand.

GenTle orb, so small and simple.

A single grain, oh wondrous sand

Who came, perhaps from a foreign land

A speck no bigger Than a pimple.

A MINDLESS EXERCISE

The locker room was just a hallway next to the gym with double doors on each end. There were two long rows of dark green lockers, and a couple of wooden benches that looked like they'd been borrowed from a cheap picnic table. The place smelled a lot like the cheese section of the supermarket.

I found a new pair of gym shorts and a shirt waiting for me in a paper bag that had *Anderson* written on it. I also found Bloodbath in the locker room, but he was busy horsing around with a couple of his buddies and stuffing one of the runts into a locker. I wondered whether he had some sort of checklist. If he did, *Hit the new kid* could be marked off for the day, along with *Cram small kid in locker*. The main thing was that I hadn't become the focus of his attention.

I was definitely ready for some exercise. There's nothing like a good sweat to make a guy feel happy. I followed the rest of the class out of the locker room and into the gym.

"That's Mr. Acropolis," Torchie said, pointing to a man standing in the middle of the floor. The guy looked like someone who used to lift weights but had given up exercise a year or two ago. His muscles were still there, but they were starting to drip.

I checked around the gym to see what we were going to play. There weren't any nets up, so it wouldn't be volleyball, and there weren't any mats, so I figured we wouldn't be wrestling.

Mr. Acropolis blew his whistle, then said, "Have a seat, class."

Everyone dropped to the floor. I figured he was going to give us some sort of talk. Maybe he'd roll out a chalkboard and teach us football plays.

I wasn't even close.

"Now breathe slowly and empty your minds," he said. Then he stopped talking while we breathed slowly and tried to empty our minds. Mine kept filling up at first, but that was sort of cool, too, since I passed a good chunk of time imagining what I could do to Bloodbath if I had a laser cannon. I saved a couple of shots for Mr. Parsons, too.

"This is gym?" I whispered to Torchie after I got tired of slicing Bloodbath into convenient pieces for easy storage.

"Yeah," he whispered back. "Kind of weird, but we get to do what we want for the last fifteen minutes."

Actually, I hated to admit it but the empty-mind thing was sort of relaxing once I got the hang of it. Of course, Flying Dan didn't stay still for long, and a couple of the others didn't seem to enjoy sitting in one place. Every five minutes or so, someone would make a farting noise. A couple of kids would laugh and Mr. Acropolis would blow his whistle. Then things would settle down for a bit. Most of the farts were fake, at least, though Hindenburg let one loose that made everybody rush to the other side of the room. Bloodbath and his friends horsed around the whole time, but the teacher didn't seem to care.

As we were finishing up, Mr. Acropolis went around telling all of us what a great job we'd done. Then he asked, "What do you want to play?"

A bunch of kids shouted, "Dodge ball!"

That was fine with me. I liked dodge ball. There's a wonderful satisfaction in smacking someone nice and hard with a fairly harmless ball. Of course, it's no fun getting smacked. But that wasn't a big problem for me. I managed to see most of the hard throws before they could hit me, and I didn't do too badly during the first game. I also made sure I was on the same side as Bloodbath. As I expected, he really liked to aim for the head, even though Mr. Acropolis kept telling everyone not to.

I got eliminated early in the second game, so I had to stand on the side of the gym and watch. Torchie was next to me. He was the first one to get out in both games. It's like he was a ball magnet. I noticed one player on the other team was really good at dodging. "Who's that?" I asked Torchie, pointing to a tall, skinny kid who didn't seem to ever get hit.

"That's Flinch," he said. "He's really good at dodge ball, but he's pretty jumpy. He usually eats with us, but he went home for the weekend."

I watched Flinch. Every once in a while, you run across a true artist. I'd known one kid, Stevie Manetti, who made the best card houses I'd ever seen. He could pile up three or four decks of cards into these great castles. Nobody else I knew even came close. And there was this girl down the block from me—she could climb trees like she was born in the woods. And, of course, I'd run across kids who did other stuff like paint or dance or play the piano.

Those kids were true artists.

So was Flinch. He was the best dodge ball player I'd ever seen. He almost always managed to get out of the way. Even after the rest of his team was blasted off the floor, he kept going. One ball—no problem. Two at once—piece of cake. Even three. Flinch jumped and twisted and ducked. The balls shot past and smacked into the wall behind him. The cool thing was that he had his hair in dozens of little braids, like a rap singer, and every time he jerked or twisted, the hair flew out like a bunch of exclamation points.

Finally, in an unusual display of teamwork, about five kids on the other side threw at once. There was no way Flinch could avoid getting hit, but he gave it a good try. He leaped and twisted, like the star of a dolphin show, but one of the balls clipped his foot.

Mr. Acropolis blew the whistle again. Gym was over. Score one for me. I'd gotten through a whole class without pissing off a teacher. Of course, Mr. Acropolis had never even given a sign that he knew I was there.

It was time for lunch next. "They do anything strange during the meal?" I asked Torchie.

"Sometimes," he said. "For a while, Principal Davis read to us while we ate. And sometimes they play music. But lunch is lunch, and there really isn't too much they can do to mess with it."

He was right. Lunch was pretty normal, except that the food was just as awful as it had been at dinner and breakfast. I guess that was normal for Edgeview. After lunch, it was time for science, which I was looking forward to, since I'd heard so much about Mr. Briggs.

THE FRACTION SONG
(TO THE TUNE OF MY DARLING CLEMENTINE)

Every fraction has two numbers
Separated by a line.
If the numerator's greater,
You can simplify it fine.

Use subtraction, use subtraction,
Or division to save time,
You'll reduce that pesky fraction.
Don't forget this little rhyme.

CHEATER ON THE PHONE AFTER LUNCH

Cheater: Hi. I can't talk long. Class starts in a minute. I just wanted to say hello.

Mrs. Woo: Are you studying hard?

Cheater: Yes, Mom.

Mrs. Woo: Your father and I will pick you up this weekend.

Cheater: Great. Hey, guess what. I met a new kid.

Mrs. Woo: Is he a nice boy?

Cheater: Yeah. Well, sort of. I think he's okay. He likes to kid me, but he's not mean. At least, not too mean. He seems pretty smart, too. Not as smart as I am, of course, but he isn't a dummy.

Mrs. Woo: Well, just be careful who you associate with.

Cheater: I will.

Mrs. Woo: How are you doing with your tests?

Cheater: I have to go. I need to get a good spot for science. Bye.

FUN WITH SCIENCE

*M*r. Briggs was waiting for us when we walked into science class. Today he was wearing a Harvard sweatshirt with his jeans. "Hey, a new face," he said. "Come on in. Welcome. Glad to have you." He smiled, and it almost looked like he meant it.

Torchie had already plunked down on the carpet next to Cheater. He took a piece of paper from his notebook and put it on the rug. I guess it was an assignment from last week. I was about to sit next to Torchie when I noticed the paper was on fire.

I guess Mr. Briggs noticed, too. He walked over and calmly stomped the paper, smothering the flame. Then he held out his hand. "Come on, give me the matches."

Torchie shook his head. "I don't have no matches." He reached into his jeans and pulled his pockets inside out. A bunch of change went flying to the floor, along with a half dozen lighters.

Mr. Briggs bent over and scooped up the lighters. "Philip, if you keep denying that you have a problem, you'll never make any progress."

"But I *don't* have no problem," Torchie said as he gathered his coins.

Mr. Briggs shook his head, then said, "I'm not going to force you to face reality. Only you can make that decision. But you might want to think about the evidence." He walked to the front of the room and started the lesson.

Torchie was right—Mr. Briggs was a pretty good teacher. And he didn't get in my face with all that new-kid garbage. But learning stuff, or not learning stuff, was never my problem. I didn't have any trouble with science or math or English—I just had trouble keeping my mouth shut sometimes. It wasn't really fair. Lots of other kids mouthed off, but I always seemed to get in the most trouble for it. My sister mouthed off sometimes, but she didn't get in trouble. Maybe it was because she was a girl. Mom always stood up for her. And Dad never got mad at her. But I didn't hold it against her. She was the only one in the family who didn't treat me like some kind of giant disappointment.

So science class was fine. Mr. Briggs pulled equipment out of the closet while he talked. I noticed that there wasn't a whole lot of stuff—just a couple microscopes, some test tubes, and a small pile of assorted junk. He showed us several experiments we could do with ropes and pulleys, then let us play around on our own. The time went pretty quickly—except for one of the runts who had the misfortune to experience thirty seconds of pure terror. I think his name was Squibly, or something like that. Bloodbath wrapped a rope around Squibly's throat and kind of lifted him up in the air, but he let go before Mr. Briggs noticed. I realized that Bloodbath was sort of like a human version of a stealth bomber—he could slip in, cause pain, and slip away without detection.

As I was leaving at the end of class, Mr. Briggs called me over to his desk. "Martin, could I talk with you for a minute?"

"Sure." I had no idea what he wanted. But he was a teacher, so he had the power to talk with me until my ears bled, if that's what made him happy.

"I've been looking over your records, and I'm a bit confused. Most of the students are here because they've had extremely serious problems in other schools. The entries in your file aren't very specific." He stopped talking and watched me.

I knew that trick. He was waiting for me to start talking. The really good interviewers on TV do the same thing. They ask a question, then they just stop talking and wait. Even after they get an answer, they wait for more. Most people can't stand silence, so they blab all their secrets away. I really wasn't in the mood to spill my life's story, so I just smiled and shrugged.

Sure enough, he couldn't stand the silence, either. "Well, I just wanted you to know that I'm here if you ever have any problems. Okay?"

"Okeydokey," I said. "Can I go now?"

"Yes. But remember, I'm here to help you." He leaned forward and gave me a warm smile.

I took a step away. "Actually, I'll bet you're here because you couldn't get a job at some big fancy college or some important chemical company." I walked off. Halfway across the room, I started to feel like a real rat. Mr. Briggs had been nice to me, and the way I'd acted, I might as well have just kicked him in the crotch. I turned around so I could say I was sorry. But he was staring out the window like his mind was a million miles away.

I sprinted down the hall and caught up with Torchie, who was just catching up with Cheater. I wondered why Cheater hadn't rushed ahead for seats. Then I noticed Bloodbath strolling along farther up the hall. I guess Cheater didn't want to risk running past him.

"He hits me every time I get near him," Cheater said, following my gaze down the hall.

"I'm not surprised." I'd suspected Bloodbath might have a couple of favorite punching bags.

"What did Briggs want?" Torchie asked.

"He wanted to let me know that I'm not really such a bad person. It was quite a relief to hear that. Guess I can pack my things and go home now."

"Really?" Cheater asked. "That's great." He grinned. Then his smile faded. "But you just got here. How come you get to leave? It's not fair."

I shook my head. This kid was amazing. He'd believe anything. He was just too easy.

"Wait. I get it," Cheater said. "You were kidding."

"Can't fool you," I told him. I looked at my schedule. "History's next. What's it like?"

Torchie grinned. Cheater grinned.

"What?" I asked.

"You'll see," Torchie said.

FORM 937-C EDGEVIEW SCHOOL

FOR OFFICIAL USE ONLY
NEW STUDENT PRELIMINARY EVALUATION FORM

Student Name: Martin Anderson

Evaluation: To be honest, I'd like to shake him up. But maybe that's my problem, not his. I sense that there's something good inside him. Not deep inside and hidden where nobody will ever find it—just inside somewhere. I'd rather not be too hasty to judge him.

Evaluator: Dale Briggs

YOU'RE HISTORY

*L*et's just say Ms. Crenshaw is big on class participation," Cheater told me.

I found out what he meant the moment I walked into the room. The teacher was right inside the doorway handing out costumes. "Hi, you must be the new boy," she said, shoving a white and fluffy bundle into my hands. "This is a voluntary class. Anyone who doesn't want to attend can choose to go to a traditional lecture with Mr. Ludovico across the hall."

I looked at my lump of fluff. It was a white wig. All I could manage to say was, "Huh?"

"You get to be Thomas Jefferson today," Ms. Crenshaw said, smiling like she'd just told me I'd won the lottery.

She handed another wig to Torchie. "You're George Washington," she said. A puff of powder drifted between his hands. Then Ms. Crenshaw thrust a folded piece of cloth toward Flinch, who grimaced and pulled away at first, but finally took it from her.

"Not Martha again," Flinch said, letting the dress flop open between his fists. "Please, I hate being Martha. I was Martha twice last week. Can't I be Ben Franklin?"

Ms. Crenshaw just kept smiling and said, "Now, that's not a very helpful attitude. Every role is important. There are no small parts. I'm sure you don't want to let the others down, do you?"

Flinch looked around. "Hey, would any of you feel let down if I didn't play Martha Washington?"

The poor kid. Once we saw how much he didn't want to play the part, there was no way we were going to help him get out of it.

"We're counting on you, *Martha*," Cheater said.

Lucky, who had just walked in, said, "Every country needs a mother. It's your duty, Flinch."

Others joined in. Flinch never had a chance. A kid might help another kid who fell into a river, and a kid might help another kid search for a lost baseball, but there isn't a kid I've met who will help another kid out of a humiliating situation. We just aren't built that way.

So I put on the wig and tried to act like Thomas Jefferson, not that I had a clue how to really do that. It was pretty much a wasted hour. We all walked around and talked about the Revolution. I'm pretty sure I didn't learn anything, except that wigs are uncomfortable.

I noticed that the tough kids who'd been in my other classes weren't in history. Ms. Crenshaw had said that there was a choice. I guess the thugs had decided they didn't want to wear costumes and wigs. As far as I was concerned, that was one good reason to stick with this class, no matter how crazy it seemed. All we had to do was walk around and make sure we used the vocabulary words the teacher had put on the blackboard. No trouble at all.

Toward the end of the period, Ms. Crenshaw asked us to sit down so we could discuss what we'd learned. I was just relaxing in my chair when someone shouted at me.

"Shut up! Just shut up!"

I looked over to my right. It was Lucky. He was glaring at me. But it was real spooky. I would have bet a thousand dollars that even though his eyes were pointed in my direction, he didn't see me.

A hand tapped my shoulder. "Don't worry about it," Torchie said. "He does that sometimes."

Nobody else seemed worried about it. I turned away from Lucky. Sure enough, a minute later, when I glanced back, he seemed okay.

At the end of the period, as I was handing in my wig, Ms. Crenshaw patted me on the arm and said, "Well, Martin, did you enjoy our little class?"

All I had to do was nod and say yes. That would have been fine. Three letters, one syllable, and I'd be out of there. Instead, I said, "You must really have a desperate desire to be in the theater." I shook my head. "This sure ain't Broadway. But it's as close as you'll ever get."

She looked like she wanted to hit me. Through gritted teeth, she said, "You don't have to participate. You can attend the lecture instead. Would you like to do that?"

I shook my head. "No thanks."

She continued to glare at me. It seemed I'd gotten another teacher to leave my fan club. That wasn't fair. I hadn't really said anything all that bad. At this rate, I'd need to start using pencil and paper to keep track of who hated me. Though with my luck, Torchie would set my list on fire.

"Does Lucky do that a lot?" I asked Torchie when we left the room.

Torchie shrugged. "Not that much. You'll get used to it. He's really a good guy. Just make sure you don't make any comments about things being missing when he's around. He's really sensitive about that 'cause he's always getting in trouble for stealing stuff."

"I'll keep that in mind." I glanced back into the room. Lucky was in the corner, reaching into the wastebasket. I couldn't tell whether he was putting something in or taking something out. I guess it didn't matter either way.

"Anyone ever get out of here?" I asked Torchie as we walked down the hall.

"Kids drop out when they get old enough," he said. "Or they get arrested and go to jail. That's only happened a couple of times, when there were real bad fights. Principal Davis doesn't like to call the cops. You can graduate, of course. But that's no good, because then you have to go to the alternative high school down in Danville. And that place is ten times worse than here."

"No, I mean does anyone ever get back to regular school?"

"There's the review," Torchie said.

"What review?" I asked.

"Didn't you read your handbook?"

I thought about the charred paper in my wastebasket. I guess I couldn't blame Torchie. Even if he hadn't set it on fire, I'd already tossed the handbook out. "Tell me about it."

"They get together at the end of your first month and discuss whether you should stay. After that, you're here for good."

"They?" I asked.

"Your teachers," Torchie said. "The ones who see you in class. It's not really fair. There were four fires the day I had my review. They blamed me. For all four! Can you believe that? I heard it was the quickest review in the history of the school."

I was only half listening to Torchie. My mind was replaying my first meeting with each of my teachers. So far, I'd pretty much guaranteed they'd hate me. One month. Maybe if I just kept my mouth shut and did my work, I'd have a chance.

There was only one class left for the day. I promised myself, no matter what, I wouldn't make another teacher angry. It turned out to be a difficult promise to try to keep.

FORM 937-C EDGEVIEW SCHOOL

———————————— FOR OFFICIAL USE ONLY ————————————

NEW STUDENT PRELIMINARY EVALUATION FOR

Student Name: Martin Anderson

Evaluation: I love them all, of course. They need me. But this one might be an exception.

Evaluator: Priscilla Nomad

GOING NOWHERE

I guess every teacher had his own idea of how to teach a class at Edgeview. Mr. Briggs obviously belonged to the crowd that thought a teacher should be a buddy and a pal. Ms. Crenshaw was really into getting the class involved. Mr. Parsons was one of those teachers who experimented with all sorts of methods. Miss Nomad seemed to think a smile and a cheerful attitude would work wonders.

Mr. Langhorn, the geography teacher, had a more traditional approach. Mr. Langhorn depended on discipline from start to finish. *Strict* discipline. As he stomped into the room, I sensed a change in everyone's mood. They had that pathetic look that a dog gets when it expects a whack on the snout with a rolled-up newspaper. Mr. Langhorn stood at his desk and glared at us for a moment. He wore his hair in a crew cut and it almost looked like he ironed his suits. I had the feeling he spent a good chunk of each day polishing his shoes.

Even though everyone was reasonably quiet, Mr. Langhorn began class by shouting, "Quiet! No more talking!" His voice was hoarse, like it had suffered from a lifetime of yelling. Little bits of spit sprayed from his mouth. I was happy the seats Cheater had grabbed for us weren't in the front row. Being close to Mr. Langhorn for a whole class would probably be a lot like taking a warm shower.

For the next hour, he filled us with geography facts. Anytime anybody fidgeted a little or whispered, Mr. Langhorn shouted. I remembered him yelling, shouting, ranting, raving, and snarling. I remembered him pointing at kids and demanding silence. I remembered him calling us all sorts of names. But I didn't remember a single fact he told us about geography—not one ocean or river or capital. I knew he talked about geography. When he wasn't yelling, he was teaching us about some country—I think it was in South America. But as hard as I tried, at the end of the period I couldn't recall a single fact he'd mentioned.

That wouldn't have been a big problem, except that as the class was ending, Mr. Langhorn strutted from desk to desk, firing questions at us. Apparently, I wasn't the only one who'd failed to absorb the lesson. Nobody came up with answers. This definitely didn't please him. By the time he got to me, he was not a happy teacher.

"You," he snapped, bending over until his face was just inches from mine. He smelled like stale tobacco and sugar-free gum. "Tell me one thing you've learned today."

I looked around the room, hoping for a clue. The walls were lined with travel posters. There were beautiful pictures of exotic places—Portugal, Singapore, New Guinea.

"Are you an idiot?" Mr. Langhorn asked. He grabbed my jaw and yanked my head back toward him. "Don't look around the room. Look at me when I'm talking to you. Did I just waste my time? Can't you give me one simple fact?" He let his hand drop from my face.

"Here's a fact," I yelled. "You've never been to any of these places. You just talk about them." It was a shot in the dark. I mean, most people don't get to travel a lot. I'd never been anywhere. For all I knew, maybe Mr. Langhorn had flown all over the world. But it was like Torchie's picture of Mars. You don't fill a room with posters of places you've been. You fill it with dreams. Still, as the words I'd just shouted echoed in my mind, I figured it wasn't something that would get me in much trouble.

Wrong again.

Mr. Langhorn got redder. He leaned closer and grabbed the edges of my desk. I expected him to pick up the desk and break it across his knee. Apparently, I'd hit on the truth, and it didn't make him happy. He stared at me for another minute. The bell rang. He stood up and backed away. "Class dismissed," he snarled.

I got up slowly. I still expected him to hit me or twist my head off. But I got out through the doorway in one piece.

"Martin, wait up."

I turned toward Mr. Briggs, who was jogging down the hallway.

"See you upstairs," Torchie said. He headed off. Cheater went the other way down the hall. I guess he was going to the library.

"Yeah?" I asked Mr. Briggs when he reached me.

"What you said before. Maybe part of that is true." He shrugged. "Maybe it's all true. But what I said was true, too. I am here if you need someone to talk to. Okay?"

"Sure." I backed up a step. Just because he understood physics and chemistry didn't mean he had any chance of understanding me. "Is that all?"

"That's all."

I made my escape and headed off toward the stairs. One thing at Edgeview was no different from any other school I'd been to—I had homework. Not a lot, but I had some math problems to do and some reading for English. From what I'd seen, at least half the kids didn't bother doing their homework, but I figured it would help kill some time. I decided to go back to the room and get started on it.

As I reached the top of the stairs, a door down the hall flew open with a bang. Nobody came out of the room. I glanced inside as I passed the open doorway. That kid Trash, the one I'd asked about in the cafeteria, was in the room, sitting at a desk, hunched over with a pencil in his hand.

Just after I turned my eyes away, I heard this fluttering whoosh, followed by a bang that made me duck and cover my head. Something had slammed into the wall right behind me, hitting hard enough to knock out a piece of plaster.

DR. STRUTHER MANDELBROT, PH.D.
DEAN OF ADMINISTRATION
SWARTHLESS UNIVERSITY
ALDENBURG, KS

Dear Ms. Crenshaw,
Thank you for your interest. We regret to inform
you that the position of Drama Teacher has been
filled. We will keep your resume on file for future
consideration.

Sincerely,

Dr. Struther Mandelbrot

Dr. Struther Mandelbrot,
Ph.D.

TORCHIE FLICKS AWAY

I spun and looked down at the math book lying on the floor. Talk about a deadly weapon. I picked it up and stared back into the room. Okay—I'd taken enough crap for one day. More than enough. I walked in. The kid glanced up, watching me with empty eyes.

"You trying to hit me?" I asked. "If you were, you'd better practice. Your aim sucks." I held out the book, ready to jump back if he took a swing at me. He was about my size—hard to tell for sure, since he was sitting—maybe a couple inches taller and a few pounds heavier, but close enough so I figured I could take him if I had to.

"I wasn't trying to hit you." He reached up, took the book from me, and tossed it on the bed. I noticed there was just one bed in the room. Torchie had told me that some of the rooms were so small they didn't try to cram two people inside.

I relaxed a bit and glanced around the room. Whoa—it looked like the inside of a rock tumbler. The window was boarded over with a sheet of plywood. There were chips of plaster missing from spots on all four walls. Most of the books in the room were piled in one corner. Tangled clothing covered the floor of the closet. The closet door was smashed through in a couple of spots and hanging from one hinge.

"You must be Trash," I said.

"I must be."

"I'm Martin," I said, holding out my hand.

"Nice to meet you."

We shook hands. His grip was a lot stronger than I expected. I took a step back. "Well, I've got homework. Better get to it."

"Okay." He turned back to his sketch pad.

I looked over his shoulder. It started out as a quick glance, but what I saw locked me in place. He was drawing this incredible scene of a rocket shooting across an alien landscape. I watched him for a few minutes, but he didn't look back up, so I went out the door and down the hall to my room.

As I got close to the room, I heard voices from inside. It sounded like Torchie and Lucky. Torchie was saying, "We can trust him."

"Maybe," Lucky said. "But I don't want to take any chances, so let's not rush."

"Okay," Torchie said.

I waited to see if they would say anything else about me, but they didn't. After a while, I felt funny standing out there listening. So I rattled the knob to make sure they heard me coming, and then went in.

"Hi," Torchie said a little too quickly.

"Hi." I sat at my desk and got started on my homework while Torchie and Lucky found another topic of conversation. It was okay if they had a secret. I was new, and it would take a while before they trusted me. I was pretty sure the secret had something to do with Friday nights, because they'd almost let something slip about that already.

A few minutes later, there was a knock on the door. Principal Davis stuck his head in and said to Torchie, "Come with me, please, Philip."

Torchie sighed as he went past me and muttered, "Didn't do nuthin'." He followed the principal out into the hallway.

"What do you think will happen to him?" I asked Lucky.

He shrugged. "No way to guess." He stared at me. I was afraid he'd start shouting again. Instead, he quietly said, "I look out for my friends. Understand? Torchie—he's my friend. Same with Cheater and Flinch. They're my friends. You treat them okay, we'll get along."

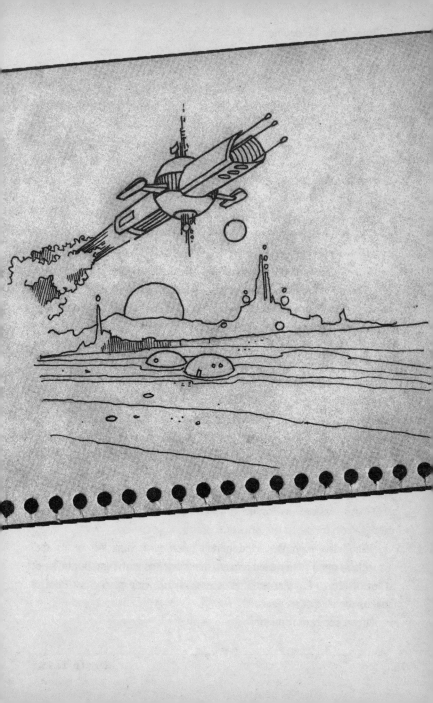

I nodded. "No problem."

He stood up. "See you later."

"Bye."

About an hour later, Torchie came back. He smelled like smoke. Well, he always smelled like smoke, but right now it was stronger than ever. "What happened?" I asked.

"They made me light fires. Can you believe that? For a whole hour, they just kept making me burn pieces of paper." He held up his right thumb. "Look. I got a blister from the lighter."

"They *made* you light fires?"

He nodded. "Guess they figured if they made me do it, I'd get tired of it. But I didn't do nothin' in the first place."

I didn't say anything. Obviously, he wanted to keep pretending that he didn't have a problem. As I finished my homework, Lucky came back. I realized that our room was the place where everyone hung out. Maybe it was because we were at the end of the hall. Maybe it was because Torchie had a lot of magazines.

Lucky had brought his portable stereo. "It's mine," he said when he caught me looking at it. "I didn't steal it. I got it last Christmas."

"Hey, I didn't say anything," I told him.

Cheater came next. Flinch dropped by soon after that. It wasn't like a party or anything—it was just a bunch of us sitting around, talking or reading or just listening to music. Maybe it was a safety thing. Together, we were less likely to be harmed by Bloodbath. Maybe it was a social thing—we had the common bond of being sent to Edgeview. I really didn't feel like trying to examine it right then.

"Does Trash ever drop in?" I asked Torchie after the other kids had left.

"Him? No way. We tried hanging out with him. All of us did. Especially me. I really tried hard to make friends with him. But he's not a lot of fun to have around. He's always throwing stuff. That kind of makes the rest of us nervous."

"I can see how it might."

Torchie shook his head. "He even threw a sneaker at Bloodbath once, in the locker room. Can you believe it? He got the crap kicked out of him for that."

I didn't want to hear any more about Bloodbath. "Hey, got anything to read besides magazines?"

Torchie pointed to the closet. "I have a ton of books in there. Help yourself."

"Thanks." I opened the closet and dug through his collection. There was a lot of good stuff. He had some Jack London and Jules Verne, but I'd already read most of that. My sister had gotten me started on them, along with H. G. Wells, Robert Heinlein, and Roald Dahl. I'd discovered Dean Koontz and Stephen King on my own. I searched around and finally picked up a battered and slightly charred paperback called *Fifty Great Science Fiction Stories*.

Maybe it was the book that gave me my first real hint. The stories I read described all kinds of strange and wonderful things. I guess they gave my mind a shove in a direction I hadn't planned. At one point, I glanced up from the book and looked at the clock on Torchie's desk. "A whole day," I said.

"What?" Torchie asked.

"I've been here a whole day."

"Happy anniversary," Torchie said.

"Thanks." I thought about my first day. It couldn't be called a success— I'd gotten nearly every teacher angry with me. I was used to that sort of reaction, but even I was surprised at how quickly I'd gotten into trouble.

Still, I didn't think it was fair to compare me with kids who set fires or stole or threw stuff or cheated all the time. *Fair*. Now, there was a fun word. Dad liked to remind me that life wasn't fair. I'd heard that from him more than once. And then he'd tell me all the things I should be thankful for, and then he'd tell me how easy my life was compared to when he was a kid. And I'd tell myself I couldn't wait to get away.

Well, here I was. Away. For real. I'd never been away from my parents like this before—not in a place I couldn't leave. I was on my own.

There were teachers all over the school—Edgeview had no shortage of adults—but that didn't change the fact that I was on my own. None of the adults here had any reason to care about what happened to me. None of the teachers was going to worry about the fate of one more face in the crowd, no matter what they might say about wanting to help. They especially wouldn't care after the way things had gone today.

As I heard the dinner bell ring, I put down the book of science fiction stories and got to my feet. "Pretty strange," I said to Torchie.

"Yeah, it's got some cool stories," he said.

I didn't bother to tell him I hadn't been talking about the book.

Memo From: Principal Davis
To: All Staff
Subject: State inspection

With our inspection just five months away, we need to begin preparations. I expect us all to pitch in and work together. Please be prepared to discuss this in detail at the next staff meeting. As you are all aware, the state has had some pressure from town residents who aren't in favor of our school. Fortunately, Mayor Walden is still on our side.

Hey Marty,

So, how's your vacation so far? Is it as much fun as the week we spent at Williamsburg? Mom and Dad miss you, even though you just left. I can tell. Well, okay, Mom misses you. Who knows what Dad's thinking. He's been stomping around all week with that angry look. You know—where he's mad but you don't have a clue why. But I sure miss you. Especially at bedtime. I still say "Good night, you creepy little twerp," but nobody answers back. I wish you'd get your act together. It feels awfully empty around here. Are you using that charming personality of yours to make any friends?

Your wonderful sister,

Teri

PART TWO

SEEING THE TRUTH

SETTLING IN

*I*f my arrival at Edgeview reminded me of a prison movie, the start of my stay reminded me of endless television reruns. My second day was distressingly like my first. I went to classes, got in trouble, and went to more classes. My second week was also pretty much like my first. In other words, I'd settled into a routine, which wasn't all that easy, since things in the classroom had a way of changing. We actually played a board game in math for a couple of days, until someone stole the dice. Mr. Langhorn tried different stuff in geography, too, but no matter what we did he always yelled. Even in history, we didn't wear costumes every day. Thank goodness. I was getting sick of the smell of talcum powder. Sometimes, we had a lecture or a test.

Miss Nomad couldn't seem to stick with one approach for more than a couple of English classes. We did worksheets for two days in a row. Then we memorized stuff for three days. That was awful. I know a preposition when I see one—I sure don't have to memorize a list of them. Then we sat and read. That was better. Then we sat and wrote, which was okay, too. Despite what I'd said to Miss Nomad, I did kinda like to write. Except when we had to do stuff about ourselves. One day she made us write an essay called, "Why I Like Being Me." Give me a break.

But, whatever we did in class, I could usually expect to be doing something else a couple days later. So, the main thing that never changed about classes was that things always changed.

Most of the time, my teachers just ignored me. That was fine. If they didn't talk to me, I didn't talk back. I figured that if I stayed as invisible as possible, they just might forget about the first day and vote to send me back to regular school when the time came for my review. I even did all my homework, though once in a while Torchie burned it before I could hand it in. There was just one problem: The teachers didn't always cooperate with my plan. Sometimes they'd slip up and ask me a stupid question. And I'd say something that would piss them off. But mostly they were learning to leave me alone.

As for my social life, it took almost three weeks—and one foolish moment on my part—before Torchie and the others shared their secret. I knew something was going on—a person would have to be as dumb as dirt not to notice all the winks, whispers, and meaningful glances they exchanged every Friday. They sure weren't playing checkers. The first Friday night after I arrived, Torchie slipped out of the room around eight. He mumbled something about going to the bathroom. He was gone for hours. If he'd spent all that time in the bathroom, there'd be nothing left of him. Torchie snuck back in around midnight, moving with all the silent grace of a moose on a floor full of marbles. I was half asleep, but I glanced at the glowing hands of his desk clock when I heard him tiptoe in from the hallway.

He repeated the scene a week later. The clumps of snow clinging to the sides of his shoes made it obvious he'd been outside. I didn't worry about it. I figured they'd tell me sooner or later. And if they didn't, it was no big deal.

I spent more time thinking about the larger puzzle that was tickling against the back of my mind. I saw a painting once that showed a couple of guys climbing a hill. At first, there was nothing special about it. But if you stepped back and let your eyes relax, the whole scene turned into a picture of a grinning skull. I felt Edgeview was like that. Whatever I saw right now, it wasn't the whole picture. I needed to step back and let my eyes drift, but I wasn't sure how to do that. At the moment, all I could do was keep my eyes open and wait for things to fall into place.

But at least I got along with my roommate and his friends, and they treated me okay. The guys even tried to give me a nickname. Flinch said they should call me Squirt because I really had a knack for pissing off the teachers. Fortunately, the name didn't stick. As smart as Cheater was, Flinch was brilliant in his own way. He didn't have a million facts in his head, but he could think up stuff really fast. Flinch saw connections. Smart or not, he got in as much trouble as the rest of us. Not only was he pretty distracted most of the time, and as jumpy as a cat in a roomful of pit bulls, but he also interrupted the teachers a lot. They tended not to appreciate that.

As for Friday nights and the big secret, I don't know how long—if ever—it would have taken before they told me. But on Wednesday of the third week I was walking down the hall when I heard the unmistakable sound of Cheater yelping in pain. I spun back and saw Bloodbath had just tossed Cheater against the wall.

"Watch where you're going next time," Bloodbath said. He grabbed Cheater with one hand and raised the other fist.

Oh boy. I knew this routine. No matter what Cheater did or said, Bloodbath would pound him for a while. I scanned the halls for the one thing that might save Cheater. No luck. There wasn't a teacher in sight. But Bloodbath didn't know that.

Trying not to think about how stupid it was to approach Bloodbath, I ran over and pointed back to the door of the nearest classroom. "Langhorn and Davis are coming out," I said, trying to fill my voice with panic. It wasn't hard.

Bloodbath flashed a smile at me. Then he punched me on the shoulder—I guess that was his way of saying thanks—and slunk away in the opposite direction.

"Thanks," Cheater said.

"Anytime."

I guess Cheater told Lucky what happened because at the end of the third week, on Friday evening, as soon as we'd gone upstairs after dinner, Torchie let me in on their secret. "Friday nights," he said, looking nervously around our room as if the walls and ceiling were filled with hidden microphones, "we do something special."

"Oh really?" I asked, trying to sound surprised.

He nodded. "Yeah. There's no way anyone would know. That's because we're real careful. We never tell anybody. But we talked about it and everyone thinks you're okay. What we do is we sneak off into town. Want to come?"

"Absolutely." My pulse sped at the possibility of getting outside of Edgeview. Even a few hours would be wonderful. We were allowed into the schoolyard, but that was as far as we could go. It almost seemed as if they were afraid to let us be seen in town. They never let us leave the school unless our folks came for us on the weekend. Mine hadn't. I was getting ready to climb the walls. "Where do you go?"

Torchie shrugged. "Usually the arcade, sometimes we just hang out."

"Sounds fine to me." Maybe I could even get a slice of pizza or some other real food. The very thought was enough to make me drool.

So that evening I learned the story of Lucky's great escape route.

WHY I LIKE BEING ME

PHILIP GRIEG

I like being me because I'm friendly. I get along ~~with~~ with everyone. Well, almost everyone who doesn't hit people, if you know what I mean. I have lots of friends. Sometimes I lose friends because their stuff gets burned up and they blame me. Even if it's not my fault. I never done nothing ~~ever done nothing~~ they say I did. But even so, I have lots of friends. Which is good. And that's the biggest reason why I like being me.

WAY OUT

Torchie whispered the whole story to me in our room. "Lucky was fooling around behind the school last October. You know, bouncing a tennis ball against the back wall. So anyhow, one time the ball got past him. When he was looking for it, he noticed this round place in the ground. He's always finding stuff. Anyhow, he decided to check it out. He got a stick and started poking around. Guess what he found?"

I shrugged. "Not a clue."

"There was this manhole cover. He called me over and we got it up. Guess what we found?"

I just shrugged again.

"A pipe," Torchie said. "This big old tunnel. I guess it was a drain or something. We followed it. I didn't really want to go, but I wasn't going to be a chicken if Lucky went. It doesn't go far, but—get this—it comes out on the other side of the fence, down at the bottom of the hill."

He paused, I guess to let me fully appreciate the meaning of that. It was the perfect way out. Since the fence was ten feet high in back, nobody ever checked to see if kids were there. They locked the front gate in the evening when the guard left.

"Which door do we use?" I asked.

Torchie shook his head. "Too dangerous. We could get caught. Lucky's room is in the back. So we go out his window."

"I thought Lucky had a room on this floor," I said.

Torchie nodded. "He does."

"But—"

"We made a ladder," Torchie said. "Lucky found some broomsticks in a closet. And we borrowed a bunch of rope from Mr. Briggs's supplies. I tied the knots myself. I was a Cub Scout. I would have been a Boy Scout, too, but I got kicked out because of this fire in my tent. Man, canvas really burns a lot faster than you'd think. But that's not important." He stood up and said, "Come on, let's get ready."

Torchie showed me how to stuff clothes under my blanket to make it look like I was asleep in bed. That was just in case anyone checked the rooms. It probably wasn't necessary. Once classes were over, nobody seemed to care all that much what we did, as long as it didn't involve too much violence or vandalism. The teachers went home in the evening, except whoever had gotten stuck with night duty, which just meant sleeping in that room on the second floor in case there was an emergency.

"One more thing," Torchie whispered as we cracked open our door. "Remember, don't ever mention stealing to Lucky. Okay?"

"Sure. No problem."

I followed Torchie down the hall to meet Lucky. True to his name, he had the room to himself. The rope ladder was already dangling out the window. A long stick tied to the top kept it from falling through. From the sharp chill in the room, it felt like the window had been open for a while. I watched as the others climbed down one at a time. When my turn came, I wasn't sure I could do it. I got my left leg out the window fine, but it took three tries before I managed to swing the other leg past the ledge.

The ladder swayed like a funhouse floor and I had to dig with my toes to get each rung away from the wall. Halfway down, my hands started to grow numb from the cold. I hurried to reach the ground before I lost my grip. Despite visions of splattering myself into a huge pile of roadkill, I made it without any real slips.

"What if we get caught?" I asked after I'd stepped away from the ladder.

Lucky shrugged. "What can they do? Shoot us?"

I saw his point. We were already at the end of the line as far as getting in trouble.

It's a good thing I wasn't afraid of the dark. Torchie had forgotten the flashlight and nobody felt like going back for it. We walked in total blackness through the pipe. It was a darkness so complete it made me feel I no longer existed except as a bundle of thoughts. Even though I wasn't scared, I didn't like the experience. It's weird what visions the mind can create when the eyes can't see. But I got through it.

The pipe spilled us out on the side of a wooded hill, about fifty yards from the road. We followed the road into town and headed for the arcade.

The thought of video games made me realize I had a problem. "I don't have any money," I told them.

"No big deal," Lucky said. He reached in his pocket and pulled out a handful of quarters.

I hesitated. It felt funny taking money from him.

"Go ahead. Help yourself. I didn't steal it." He shook his hand, jangling the coins in his palm.

"I never said you did. It's just that I don't know when I can pay you back." I figured I could ask my folks for some money, but they probably wouldn't send me any.

"Don't worry about it," Lucky said. "It's my treat. You want it or not?"

"Thanks." I took the coins from him and put them in my pocket.

The town of Edgeview wasn't very big. Actually, the main part was across the interstate. The side we could reach was only about seven blocks from the school, but traveling through town felt like walking into a different world—a world of houses, homes, and families.

It didn't take long to figure out that I was marked. Groups of kids, standing and horsing around in the streets, got quiet when we went past. Some of them crossed the street when we came near. A couple little kids even ran away from us.

"What's going on?" I asked Torchie.

"Huh?" He looked around as if he didn't know what I meant. Maybe he was used to seeing kids flee from him.

"They're scared of us," Cheater said, grinning. "Can you believe that? They think everyone from Edgeview is dangerous. Do I look like a killer?"

I squinted at him. "Hard to tell in the dark. Take off your glasses and try to look mean."

He had his hand halfway to his face before he realized I was kidding.

I wondered how the kids from town knew we were from Edgeview.

"It's a small place," Cheater said, as if he'd guessed my next question. "So we really stick out. They know we don't go to the public school. They call us 'Alters,' since we go to the Alternative School."

"Guess what we call them?" Flinch asked.

"I give up. What?"

"Edgies," Flinch told me. "I came up with that."

I wasn't surprised. Flinch had a gift for funny stuff. He was the one who'd started calling Waylon *Hindenburg*.

"You'll get used to them," Cheater told me. "Hey, I'm certainly used to people treating me different. When everyone stares at you, after a while it's like nobody at all is staring."

"That's the truth," Flinch said.

I guess they had a point. But it really felt strange the way the town kids acted. I'd wondered how they'd react to someone who was really dangerous, like Bloodbath. He'd plow through these kids like a bulldozer through a basket of light bulbs.

As we got closer to the small strip mall, I scanned the stores, hoping for a pizzeria or a burger place. No luck. There was a video store at the end nearest us. I guess it closed early, because the lights were off. I realized I hadn't seen a movie in weeks. Past that store, a laundry pumped the steamy smell of clothes dryers into the air. The drugstore next to it had a sign in front that said NO LOITERING. Beyond the drugstore, jangling and flashing in that unmistakable way, stood the arcade. It was called MondoVideo. Nice surprise—it was larger than I'd thought it would be. I went inside, expecting nothing more than a few hours of fun.

But it was in the arcade, surrounded by the bright noise of mindless electronic entertainment, that I began to see the whole picture.

TWO EDGIES TALKING ON THE SIDEWALK A BLOCK FROM THE ARCADE

Edgie One: Oh man, it's Alters.

Edgie Two: Let's get out of here. Those guys will beat up anyone they get their hands on. [he starts to run]

Edgie One: [running] I hope they don't follow us.

Edgie Two: I heard some of them carry knives.

Edgie One: [panting and looking back] It's okay. They didn't follow us.

Edgie Two: That was close. I hate those guys.

Edgie One: Don't worry. I heard the place is getting shut down.

A GLIMMER OF THE TRUTH

I'm not a bad game player. I do best at the driving games, but I do okay on the other stuff, too. And I like pinball. Torchie, Cheater, and Lucky were all pretty good, but Flinch came close to being amazing. I started out playing Road Revenge. Flinch was standing next to me, taking on one of the new fighting games with the really cool graphics. Out of the corner of my eye, I noticed he was undefeated after I'd already gone through a dollar. That got my attention. In the next hour, I saw him roll up incredibly high scores at almost every game he played. I could barely believe that someone who was so jumpy could play games so well.

"He's got great reflexes," Torchie said as we watched Flinch blast his way through level after level on Smash TV. They had a lot of the latest stuff at the arcade, but Flinch seemed to like the old games as much as the new ones. He'd go from something brand-new like Shaolin Annihilator to something ancient like Pole Position, Frogger, or Centipede. I stuck with the old games, since most of them were still just a quarter. I didn't want to run through Lucky's money too quickly. I even played a game of Skee Ball for old times' sake, hitting just enough of a score to win one ticket. My sister and I used to play it when we were little. I usually gave her all the tickets I won so she could save up for good prizes. I shoved the ticket in my pocket, figuring I could send it to her as a joke.

I beat my old high score on Xenon, one of my favorite pinball machines. For a moment, as I stood there, just drinking in the great sounds that washed over me from all the machines, life seemed absolutely fine.

Flinch stepped away from Smash TV and went to one of the all-time pinball classics—Eightball Deluxe.

"Want to play a two-player game?" Torchie asked me, pointing to NBA Jam.

I shook my head. Right then, I just wanted to watch Flinch. There was something odd about the way he used the flippers.

"Guess I'll play pinball," Torchie said, stepping up next to Flinch and feeding some change into Excalibur.

I think, if I'd just watched Flinch, I might never have noticed what was going on. But with Flinch and Torchie standing side by side, I began to see the differences in the ways they played.

After a while, I started to understand what Flinch was doing. As the first suspicions grew, a shiver of excitement tingled across my flesh. Beneath the thrill of discovery was a tinge of fear.

Even though I was sure I'd figured out what was happening, I didn't quite believe it.

A couple minutes before midnight, the lights blinked on and off. "Closing time," the guy behind the counter shouted.

"We'd better get going," Torchie said.

It was just as well—I was down to my last three quarters. "Here," I said, handing them to Lucky.

"Keep 'em," he told me.

I felt funny about that. "I don't need—"

"Keep the quarters, okay?" He glared at me, his hands clenched in fists.

"Yeah. Sure. Thanks." I wasn't going to get into a fight over it. If he wanted me to have the quarters that badly, I'd keep them.

We headed out. I watched Flinch carefully on the way back to the school. He didn't do anything unusual, but I decided to keep an eye on him.

We got inside without any trouble. Much to my surprise, climbing up was a lot less scary than climbing down. As Lucky hauled in the ladder and stuck it under his bed, my eyes homed in on the open closet.

"Wow." I couldn't help gasping. There was no way the door could close. The closet was crammed with stuff. I stared at stacks of cardboard boxes overflowing with an amazing variety of loot—pens, eyeglasses, tape recorders, hats, wallets, all kinds of small toys. I saw at least a dozen baseballs, most pretty scuffed but one that looked brand-new, a bunch of golf balls, tons of tennis balls, and a jar full of coins.

"Found 'em," Lucky said. "I didn't steal them."

"All of that?" I walked over to the boxes.

"Yeah, all of that. Especially around home on the weekends." His voice grew tense. He moved a step closer to me. "I found it all. Finders keepers."

"Great." I held my breath, hoping he wasn't going to get angrier.

Lucky smiled. "Go ahead. Take anything you want."

I looked at him, unsure what to say.

He nodded. "Really."

I figured he'd get upset if I refused. I reached toward the top box. It felt funny—almost like I was stealing. But Lucky started to look tense again so I just grabbed the first thing my hand touched. "Thanks. This is great," I said. I looked down and discovered I was holding one of those big plastic clips girls use in their hair.

"Nice choice, Martin," Flinch said. "Maybe we can get you a dress to go with it." He started laughing, and exchanged a hand slap with Torchie.

"Hey—I'm going to send it to my sister," I said. I shoved the stupid thing in my pocket and left the room. Sometimes, Flinch just didn't know when to keep his mouth shut.

"That was fun, wasn't it?" Torchie asked after we'd slipped back into our room.

"Yeah. Thanks for letting me come." I thought about telling him what I'd seen, but I decided to wait until I had real proof.

It wasn't as simple as I'd hoped. After spending most of Saturday trying to study Flinch without being obvious about it, and learning absolutely nothing, I realized it might be better to get more information first. So I decided to do some research. If I was right, everything I knew about the world was about to change. Everything I knew about the whole universe, for that matter.

After breakfast Sunday morning, while all my classmates were hanging out and relaxing, or spending quality time at home with their parents, I went to the school library down on the first floor. The librarian—I think it was the same guy who taught the history lecture—seemed shocked to see someone. Or annoyed that I had disturbed his nap. I'm not sure which. Either way, I had the place pretty much to myself.

I wasn't exactly sure where to start, so I wandered around reading the titles of books on the shelves. I knew I could look something up on the computer catalog that listed all the books in the library, but I didn't even know what to look under. It was like trying to find a word in the dictionary when you didn't know how to spell it. But at least the library didn't have as many books as the dictionary had words.

"Can I help you?" the librarian asked after I'd scanned the shelves for ten minutes or so. He walked over toward me, but stopped several feet away, as if I might be contagious. I guess it drove him crazy watching me search the shelves like someone trying to find the right variety of soup in the supermarket.

"No thanks, I'm just looking."

He gave me that special smile teachers use with students who aren't very bright. "Well, if you tell me what you're looking for, I can help you find it."

I shrugged. "I won't know what I'm looking for *until* I find it."

"Suit yourself. But call me if you need help."

"I will." I resumed my search. There was a lot of interesting stuff. There were some books about dinosaurs and tanks and outer space. All the books looked pretty worn. The ripped covers were wrapped in yellowing plastic. A lot of them were patched with tape that had turned stiff and brittle. I flipped open a couple of the books and checked the dates. Most of them were written years ago. I guess an old book is just as good as a new one if it has the facts you need. But at first I didn't see anything that would do me any good.

Then I got warm. I spotted a book called *A Skeptical Look into the World of the Unexplained*. That seemed worth a shot. I took it to one of the tables and started flipping through the pages.

The guy who wrote the book talked about all kinds of unexplained phenomena like ghosts and stuff, and he tried to explain them in normal terms. Some of the unexplained stuff he'd investigated was obviously fake. He'd caught people making thumping sounds and pretending it was a ghost, or using hidden springs to make objects jump off a shelf. There were all kinds of frauds out there. Some of them were after money, and some just wanted attention.

I wasn't interested in the fakes. The most important thing I got from the book was a list of the words for what I wanted to learn about. I'd brought a notebook with me. I wrote down the words—*clairvoyance, telepathy, telekinesis,* and several others. Then I went to the computer— it was an old piece of junk with a green screen, and the software was pretty lame, but it had all the books in the library on file so you could search for titles and subjects. I noticed the librarian giving me a smug look, like he'd won some sort of contest. I ignored him.

I searched the computer for the words I'd found. There weren't any books on the subjects. That didn't surprise me. It wasn't the sort of thing a school library would have. So I tried the encyclopedia. Bingo. I found short articles under several of the words. And I learned a couple more words from those articles, especially the part at the end where they say *see also*. I added those words to the bottom of my list. After I'd looked at everything I could find in the encyclopedia, I took those new words and went back to the computer. This time, I actually found two books listed.

As much as I hate to admit it, I was starting to have fun in the library. If I told the guys that I was enjoying myself, I'd be kidded without mercy. They'd probably start calling me Bookman or Wordboy, or something like that. I certainly wasn't a brain, and I didn't think of myself as the kind of kid who studies stuff or learns things just for fun, but this was almost as good as a game.

And I'd done it all by myself. I'd gone in there with little more than a suspicion, and ended up learning a lot more than I'd expected. As I sat back in the chair at the library, thinking about all I'd read and what I suspected, I realized there was an easy way to get the proof I needed. And I could do it before the end of the day.

Hey Marty,
Guess what? I think Dad misses you. Actually, I think he misses having you to yell at. So he's been yelling at Mom. She doesn't yell back, of course, but she's been getting even by burning dinner. How's it going out there? I hope you're getting better meals than I am. I think it's time I learned to cook.

Your marvelous sister,
Teri

MILKING THE MOMENT

I was in the library so long, I missed lunch. I guess the bell rang, but I didn't pay any attention to it. So I had to wait until dinner to spring my trap. It was tough keeping quiet. The guys would be blown away when I told them what I'd figured out. It was all so amazingly incredible. I caught up with them in line. Lucky hadn't come back from his weekend with his dad, so it was just Flinch, Torchie, Cheater, and me.

When we brought our trays out from the food line, I grabbed a seat next to Flinch. This was perfect. All I needed was a distraction.

That came quickly enough. I noticed Torchie's napkin was on fire. It wasn't a big blaze—the edge was lightly smoldering. "Fire," I said, just loud enough so Flinch looked at Torchie's tray. I reached out and smothered the fire with my right hand. As I leaned across the table, I knocked over my milk with my left hand.

Before the carton even landed on its side, Flinch jumped out of his seat. At that point, he still wasn't looking in my direction.

"Hey, careful," he said as the milk glugged out of the open lip of the carton and splashed over the spot where his butt had just been resting.

"Wow. I'm sorry," I said. I mopped up the chair with a handful of extra napkins I had on my tray. I knew I'd need them, so I'd grabbed a whole bunch. It was hard to keep from grinning. But I wasn't grinning over spilled milk, I was grinning over the proof I'd hoped to find. As I'd expected, Flinch was bone dry—not a drop had touched him.

"What's so funny?" he asked.

"I'll tell you later," I whispered. This was great. I was dying to tell them right there, but I didn't want anyone at the other tables to hear. "It's a secret. I'll explain when we get back to the room."

"I can't wait to hear this," Flinch said.

"Hear what?" Torchie asked.

"Later," I said.

Cheater gave me an odd look. I had a feeling he already knew what I was going to talk about. Even so, he didn't say anything. None of the others had a clue yet. But that would change after dinner.

As I finished my meal, I thought about how thrilled they'd be to hear the truth.

"Okay," Torchie said after we'd had gathered in the room. "What's this big mystery?"

That was a good choice of words. I felt like the detective at the end of a mystery movie, when he's gathered all the suspects together and is about to explain everything. I stood up and pointed at Cheater. "Why are you at this school?"

"You know why," he said. "They think I cheat on tests."

"Do you cheat?"

"No. I don't need to cheat. I'm smart. Ask me anything. Anything at all."

"I know you're smart," I told Cheater. "What about you? Why are you here?" I asked, pointing to Flinch.

"I'm kind of jumpy," he said. "I guess I get distracted a lot. It messes up my grades. According to my teachers, I'm *a disruptive influence in the classroom.*"

"And we all know why Torchie is here," I said. "But maybe the adults are wrong about you guys. Maybe there's another explanation." This was going to be great. They'd be amazed when I told them what I'd figured out.

"What explanation?" Torchie asked.

Here goes, I thought. "You all have psychic abilities."

Dead silence filled the room and three pairs of puzzled eyes stared at me. I might as well have been speaking Turkish. I realized they needed more of an explanation. I could understand that. This was a big idea to grasp all at once. "Flinch has precognition and Cheater is telepathic," I said, stumbling a bit over the words as I showed off my new vocabulary. I waited for them to congratulate me on my brilliance.

"Huh?" Torchie said.

"Precognition?" Flinch asked. "Sounds like a device that starts a car by remote control."

Cheater just looked at me like I was crazy.

"Really," I said. "It's true. Cheater is telepathic. He can read minds. That's why he always has the same answers on his tests as other people in the room. I'll prove it."

I needed to concentrate on something so Cheater could read my mind. A number—that would be a good test. But not a small number. It couldn't be something simple like the number seven. Everyone thinks of seven. Just like everyone thinks of the ace of spades if you ask them to name a card. It had to be a bigger number. My house was on 85 Pritchard Drive. I closed my eyes and thought real hard of the number eighty-five. I pictured a big eighty-five—huge, red digits flashing like a score in a video game. I said, *Eighty-five, eighty-five, eighty-five*, over and over in my mind, then asked, "Okay, Cheater, what number am I thinking of?"

"How should I know?" Cheater said.

"Come on, take a guess." I knew he could get it.

Cheater shrugged, then said, "Seven. Is that it?"

"Yeah. I mean, it was, but then I changed it. It started out as seven."

"Big deal," Flinch said. "Everyone picks seven."

"Forget about the numbers. That doesn't matter. Think back," I urged the others. "Cheater always knows what I'm thinking. It must have happened to the rest of you, too. Haven't any of you noticed? Come on, you must have."

"My mom usually knows what I'm thinking," Torchie said.

"I'm thinking you blew a brain gasket," Flinch said.

I could tell they were ready to walk away. This was not how it was supposed to go. They should have been thrilled. They should have been thanking me. Maybe Cheater wouldn't cooperate, but I wasn't ready to give up.

"Flinch," I said, pointing at him. "I know this sounds really wild, but you're precognitive. That means you know things are going to happen before they happen. Like with the milk. You jumped before I spilled it."

"You did that on purpose?" Flinch asked, his face shifting from surprise to anger. "Hey, that's really rotten. I could have gotten all wet."

"But you didn't. That's the point. Why do you think you're so jumpy? It's because you see stuff coming before it happens. You knew the milk was going to spill. Somehow, you saw it before it happened, or felt it, or just knew it was coming. The rest of us, we go through life getting bumps and having small accidents. I'm always stubbing my toes. Or I'll bang my elbow when I walk around a corner. You avoid all that, but it makes you look real jumpy. And you start worrying about all the stuff you see coming from the future instead of paying attention to the present."

I paused to catch my breath. I felt like I was giving a speech, but I couldn't help myself. There was so much to tell them. "You get in trouble for interrupting, too. You think the teacher's done talking, but that's 'cause you're seeing ahead. Or hearing ahead. Don't you get it? It makes perfect sense."

Flinch shook his head. "I just can't believe you spilled that milk on purpose."

"It doesn't make sense at all," Cheater said. "And Flinch is right, it wasn't nice of you to spill milk on him."

I ignored Cheater and revealed my final piece of evidence. "Think about Torchie," I said. "Have you ever seen him actually light a fire? Even once? I haven't. And I live in the same room with him. They're always blaming him, but nobody's ever caught him. He'd have to be the sneakiest kid ever born to get away with that. Torchie isn't sneaky. He's telepyric. That means he can start fires with his mind." I grabbed my notebook, ripped out a page, and thrust the sheet of paper at Torchie.

"Come on, light it."

"Martin," Torchie said. "This is some kind of stupid joke, right?"

"No joke. Come on, light it." I moved the paper right in front of his face. "Please."

"I can't do nuthin' like that. Honest. I told you I didn't start no fires."

"You didn't know you started them," I said. "But you caused the fires—not with a lighter, but with your mind. Come on, try. If you're my friend, you'll at least give it a shot."

Despite his protests, Torchie tried. He stared at the paper. His brow got all wrinkled. His eyes narrowed to slits. He concentrated so hard that he grunted.

Nothing happened.

"Are you sure you're trying?" I asked.

"Yeah, I'm trying. It's not working. Face it, Martin. You're crazy. How's that for a simple explanation? Edgeview has gotten to you."

"Yeah, Edgeview has pushed you over the edge," Flinch said. "How's the view from there?"

"I'm not crazy," I told them. "It all makes sense—perfect sense. Think about it."

"It's getting late," Cheater said. "It's almost eighty-five."

"What did you say?" I spun toward him. A tingle of excitement ran through my scalp as his words sunk in. *Eighty-five.*

FROM THE FRANKLIN CONCISE ENCYCLOPEDIA
(1963 EDITION)

Telepathy, also known as mind reading, is the theoretical ability to sense the thoughts of others. Though many claims of telepathic ability have been made over the centuries, no scientific evidence has been found.

See also: parapsychology, extrasensory perception.

BELIEVE ME ALONE

Cheater pointed to his watch. "I said it's nearly eight thirty-five."

"No, you said *eighty-five*. That was the number I was thinking of. Really. Look, I can prove everything. We can set up some tests. Okay?" I'd read about all kinds of tests for psychic abilities. Some of the tests used these cards with different patterns on them. I figured I could do the same thing with a regular deck.

If Cheater could tell what card I was looking at, that would prove he could read minds. And if Flinch could tell what the next card was before I turned it over, that would prove he could see the future. As for Torchie, all he had to do was set the deck on fire. "I'm sure someone has cards. Let me find cards and I'll show you."

"Maybe tomorrow," Cheater said as he walked toward the door.

"Yeah, I'm outta here," Flinch said. He started to follow Cheater. Then he jumped back. At that instant, Cheater yanked at the door real hard. It flew open and the knob slipped from his hand. If Flinch hadn't jumped, he'd have gotten hit.

"See!" I shouted, pointing at Flinch.

Flinch glanced back at me. "See what? Nothing happened. Forget about it, Martin. It's not funny."

I watched them leave, then plunked down on my bed. "It's true," I said to Torchie. "Every single word I said is true. I looked it all up. It's in the books." I couldn't understand why Cheater had gotten so angry.

It didn't make any sense at all. Maybe Flinch was angry about the milk. Okay. I could see that. But still, the stuff I was trying to tell him was way more important than a pair of wet pants.

Torchie sighed. "It would be nice if you were right," he said. "I really didn't start those fires. Honest."

"I know," I told him. "That's what I've been trying to explain. But everyone acted like I was out of my mind. Don't you see—this means you didn't do anything bad. At least, not on purpose. You and Flinch and Cheater aren't like the other kids at Edgeview. You don't belong here. You're innocent." If I could convince Torchie, I figured I could get him to help me with the others.

But Torchie glared at me. "So the only person who believes me is a crazy kid. And he thinks I'm some kind of freak who can start fires with my mind. Wonderful. Maybe I can get a job in a circus." He dropped down in his chair and picked up a magazine.

"But . . ." I didn't know what else I could say to convince him. For a moment, I sat on the edge of my bed and watched Torchie. As he read, I could have sworn that I saw a small wisp of smoke rise up from the front cover of the magazine right where he held it. Maybe it was my imagination. I sniffed the air. There seemed to be a faint burnt odor, but our room always smelled like that. I kept watching, but there was no more smoke.

Why didn't he believe me? It was so obvious. I thought about all the time I'd spent in the library. Couldn't they see I was trying to help them out? I'd even missed lunch for them. The least they could do was think about what I'd said. And Torchie—who claimed to be my friend—had let me down the worst. All he had to do was start one stinking little fire while the others were watching and they'd know that I was right. One lousy stinking little fire—that wasn't a lot to ask. But he hadn't done it.

I looked at him, sitting there with his stupid magazine, moving his lips as he read. It was amazing—he was actually stumbling through life totally unaware of his abilities. I got off the bed and walked over to him. There had to be some way to make him understand. When I opened my mouth, the wrong thing came out. "If you were smart, you'd believe me," I told him. "But I guess you're not very bright. Face it—you're probably not even smart enough to be called stupid. You'd need another ten or twenty IQ points to reach that level."

Torchie threw down his magazine. He looked like he wanted to stand up and take a swing at me. I almost hoped he would. But he just said, "I'm as smart as I need to be." He stared at me as if daring me to say another word.

I kept my mouth shut. Torchie picked up his magazine and went back to reading. I crossed the floor, flopped on my bed, and turned toward the wall. The silence in the room grew heavier with every passing minute, broken only by the rustle of each page that Torchie turned. The crinkle of the paper reminded me of the crackle of a fire.

I knew I'd been wrong to say those things to him. Wrong and rotten. Just thinking about it made me feel guilty. I took a deep breath, then told him, "I'm sorry."

"That's okay." He still sounded hurt. I knew it wasn't really okay. He didn't say anything else, and I didn't know what to say to him.

Damn. What was wrong with me? I couldn't even fit in with the freaks and misfits. After Torchie and the others had let me into their group so quickly, I figured things might be okay here. It was my own fault—I'd been stupid enough to believe I'd make friends. I sat on my bed and looked around. Torchie was just a few feet from me, and dozens of other kids were right down the hall. There were kids everywhere, but I'd managed to end up alone. *Way to go, Martin*. From the moment I'd gotten to Edgeview, Torchie had been friendly. Now he didn't even want to look at me. I stood up and let my eyes wander around the room. The wall above my bed was bare and empty. There was hardly any sign that someone besides Torchie had lived in this space during the last three weeks.

"I'm going out," I said.

He didn't answer.

I left the room and walked down the hall, looking at the closed doors lining both sides of the corridor and knowing I had no place to go. Nobody wanted to see me. Nobody cared.

It felt almost like being at home.

IN THE CAR COMING BACK TO EDGEVIEW

Lucky: Mind if I turn on the radio?

Mr. Calabrizi: As long as it isn't that modern stuff.

Lucky: Oldies?

Mr. Calabrizi: Sure.

Lucky: Hey, that new kid I told you about last month. Remember?

Mr. Calabrizi: No.

Lucky: You know, the one in Torchie's room?

Mr. Calabrizi: Right.

Lucky: I think he might be okay. I wasn't sure at first, but he seems like an okay guy. I'd trust him on my side if things got tough.

Mr. Calabrizi: If things get tough, leave the room. Besides, if he's okay, what's he doing at Edgeview?

Lucky: Hey. What about me? I'm there.

Mr. Calabrizi: [sighing] I know.

IF I TOLL YOU ONCE

*I*f I was walking away from a bad situation, I was walking into one that was worse. I realized my mistake halfway down the hall when I came face-to-face with Bloodbath and three of his gang—Grunge, Lip, and the guy with the skull tattoo on his forehead.

"Hey, this is a toll road," Bloodbath said, holding his hand out. "Pay up."

"I don't have anything," I told him, taking a step back.

Grunge and Lip took two steps forward. "Everyone has something," Bloodbath said.

Before I could move, Grunge grabbed me in a headlock. The sharp, ripe smell of his unwashed shirt smacked me like a punch to the nose. I tried to pull away, but his arm tightened, locking around me like a giant handcuff. Lip and Skullface flipped my pockets inside out. Three quarters dropped to the floor, followed by a fluttering green rectangle. I tried not to stare at it.

"Nothing?" Grunge asked, tightening his grip around my neck. "That don't look like nothing."

Lip scooped up the quarters and handed them to Bloodbath.

"Next time you lie to me," Bloodbath said, "I'll break something. Understand?"

"Yeah."

Bloodbath glanced down at the floor. Since yesterday when I'd shoved it in my pocket at the arcade, I'd forgotten all about the ticket.

"What's that?" Bloodbath asked, tapping the ticket with the toe of his sneaker.

I came within a breath of saying, *It's from the arcade*. But I couldn't. I'd given my word to keep the secret. Even after the way Torchie and the others had treated me, I wasn't going to rat them out. At least the ticket had fallen facedown, so it wasn't obvious that it was an arcade ticket. I tried to remember what was written on the front.

"Hey!" Grunge snapped, squeezing my neck so hard that things started to turn gray. "The man asked you a question."

If he caught me lying, I was dead. "It's my lucky ticket," I said. "I've had it for years."

They all laughed. "Doesn't seem to be working very well," Bloodbath said.

He must have given some signal, because Grunge unclamped his arms from my neck. But Grunge wasn't quite done. Instead of just letting me go, he pushed me hard. I was already off balance. I staggered and fell.

"Man, this job pays lousy," Bloodbath said, jingling the quarters in his hand as he walked away.

I glared after them, then reached out and turned the ticket over. On the front, in giant letters, it said, *MondoVideo*. I shoved it back in my pocket.

As much as I didn't want to return to the room, it seemed safer than staying in the hall. It wouldn't be very pleasant to be around if Bloodbath wandered back. There really wasn't any choice. I headed to the room.

Torchie didn't even look up when I came in. It was obvious he

didn't want to talk. If he knew what I'd just been through—if he knew how well I'd kept his secret—maybe he'd feel differently.

I tried to think of some way to tell him. But I couldn't think of any way to start. In my mind, I saw myself talking and I saw him just staring, not really caring what I said.

I don't care, either, I told myself as I went to sleep. Right. Unlike Bloodbath, I didn't believe my lies.

Memo To: All Staff
From: Principal Davis
Subject: State evaluation

With our inspection just slightly more than four months away, we need to finalize our preparations. This is too crucial to leave for the last minute.

NOW YOU SEE ME, NOW YOU DON'T

Cheater and Flinch ignored me the next day. Torchie also pretty much acted like I didn't exist. I don't know what they told Lucky, but seeing how he already wasn't my biggest fan, he seemed happy to go along with them.

I was sitting in math class, thinking about how rotten my former friends were, when Parsons walked up to my desk and said, "Well, Anderson, do you have your homework or don't you?"

The words left my mouth like buckshot. "Well, Mr. Parsons, do you have a hairline or don't you?"

He grabbed the edge of my desk. "You have detention today, you wise-mouthed little snot. That's what you have." He glared at me, daring me to say more.

It would have been smart to keep quiet. But I couldn't control myself. I was so angry I didn't even try. "Hey, what ever happened to sticks and stones?" I asked. "You shouldn't let a few little words bother you. Isn't that part of your job? Aren't you supposed to know how to deal with little snots like me? Can't you handle me?"

He stood up and backed away a step, his eyes saying he'd be happy to rip off my arms and beat me over the head with them. "Make that a week's detention."

"Fine." I didn't care. Detention didn't matter. I'd just have to sit at a desk for an hour and be quiet. Which would be pretty much like hanging around in my room with Torchie, the way he was treating me.

I slithered out of math at the end of the period and went to English, hoping I could sulk in peace. No such luck. As soon as the class started, Miss Nomad walked over with my essay and said, "Martin, you did a wonderful job on your assignment. Would you like to share your little composition with the class?"

Why couldn't they just leave me alone? "Not really, but I'd bet they'd sure as hell rather hear my little composition than one of your drippy little poems."

Man, that was pretty brutal, even by my standards. I thought she was going to take my head off. Of course, she'd do it with a smile. But she whirled away from me and stormed to the front of the room. She didn't even give me detention.

Then Mr. Acropolis slammed me against a wall in gym class. I don't remember what I'd said to him. Apparently, he'd found our conversation displeasing. The back of my head bounced off the wall and everything got kind of blurry for a moment. My head was still ringing when I went into the locker room. I think Bloodbath hit me, too, but I'm really not sure. By then, I just wanted to find a hole where I could bury myself.

As rotten as my morning had been, lunch started out just as awful. I found myself stranded at the end of the cafeteria with a tray full of food and not a clue where to sit. All the seats were filled at Torchie's table. The empty chairs had been shoved aside. I could have brought over a chair. But, given how they'd been treating me, I didn't want to take any chances. If I walked over and they didn't let me join them, the whole cafeteria would see me getting shut out.

I scanned the cafeteria, hoping to spot a friendly face. There was no way I was going to sit by myself. The other choices didn't look very appealing. I couldn't join Bloodbath's group. They'd chew me up and spit me out like a mouthful of mashed turnips. And I certainly wasn't going to sit with the runts.

That's when I found myself walking toward Trash. Why not? Maybe everyone would think I was sitting there as a joke, just having some fun with him. That would work.

He didn't look up as I pulled out a chair across from him. I wondered whether I should say something, but all that ran through my mind was pointless chatter. *Is this seat taken?* Talk about a stupid question. He'd been surrounded by empty chairs from the start. *Mind if I join you?* Too risky. If he said no, I'd look like a real moron. *Break anything interesting lately?* Right. So I just sat down.

Trash's eyes flickered toward me, but he stayed hunched over his food.

"Hi," I said, feeling awkward. There was still the possibility he'd ask me to leave.

"Hi." That's all he said to me. No welcome, no suggestion that I get lost. Just a "hi." Sadly, it was the nicest conversation I'd had so far that day.

I didn't bother trying to talk any more. I ate my lunch, struggling to get the food past a throat that wanted to close tighter with each swallow. I'd sat with my back to Torchie, so I couldn't even tell what those guys were doing, but I was sure they were amused to see me at Trash's table. I could just imagine what they were saying.

As I was finishing my lunch, I was startled from my thoughts by a clatter of metal against linoleum. Trash had thrown his fork to the floor. "Why'd you do that?" I asked.

Trash didn't offer any explanation. No big deal. As long as he didn't stick his silverware into me, I really didn't care what else he did with it. He could sit on his fork and spin in circles if that made him happy.

The bell rang.

I passed Torchie on the way out, just to see if he'd say anything. There was no harm giving him a chance to apologize. But he ignored me.

I mouthed off to Mr. Briggs in science. He didn't look too thrilled, but he let it go. Ms. Crenshaw wasn't as reasonable. She kicked me out of class and sent me across the hall to the lecture.

I almost made it through geography. The class was nearly over when Mr. Langhorn started walking around the room, quizzing us on capitals. He marched up to me, an open book in his hand, leaned over, and shouted, "BURMA!"

I hated the way he shouted. At least all I had to do to get him off my back was to say, *Rangoon.* I knew that stuff. I'd learned most of it back in seventh grade. Instead of answering, I reached out and slammed the book shut, right between his hands. He looked so startled, I thought his eyebrows would fly off toward the ceiling.

I couldn't stop.

"TIBET?" I shouted. "Go ahead. Tell us. Can you name capitals without that book of yours? Come on. What's the capital of Tasmania? Too hard? How about Argentina?"

Mr. Langhorn threw the book down. "You arrogant little beast," he said, pointing a shaking finger at me. "You'll be severely punished for this." He stomped back to his desk and wrote something on a piece of paper. "Take this to the office," he ordered, shoving the slip at one of the runts.

I heard a couple of kids chuckling. Langhorn did look pretty funny. I glanced over at Torchie. He started to smile. Then I guess he remembered he wasn't talking to me because he turned away. Cheater looked away, too, but not before mumbling, "Lhasa," to show everyone he knew the capital of Tibet.

After class, I reported to the detention room. It wasn't crowded. From what I'd seen, a kid had to just about commit murder to win detention. Most of the students were so out of control already that the teachers just put up with them.

I hadn't been there for more than five minutes when Principal Davis showed up. "Come along, Martin," he said. "We have a special program for you."

He smiled at me. It was one of the scariest expressions I'd ever seen.

Memo From: Principal Davis
To: All teaching staff
Subject: Corporal punishment
Please note the following revisions to our punishment policy.

---

1. Physical punishment is allowed when deemed necessary, but must be administered under the following guidelines.
    A. Strikes must be made only with an open hand.
    B. Do not hit easily breakable areas such as the nose.
    C. Paddles are permitted.
    D. Do not use any other hard objects.

2. We are investigating various methods, all of which have been approved at the state level.

3. Bear in mind that there must be a purpose to any punishment. If we strike out in anger, we are teaching the students to strike out in anger.

CURRENT METHODS

We didn't go far.

The small room at the end of the hall past the principal's office was amazingly ordinary. It looked like it might have been a storage area at one time. A single chair in the middle of the floor faced a pull-down movie screen on the left wall. The window opposite the door was covered with a heavy shade. Behind the chair, set slightly to one side, was a table holding a slide projector.

"Have a seat," Principal Davis said.

I sat. He reached under the arm of the chair and fastened a leather strap around my wrist. A wire ran from the strap. I could feel bare metal pressing against my skin.

"Now, Martin, we're going to play a little game. I'm going to show you a picture, and you are going to say something nice."

"Okeydokey," I said, speaking quickly so my words wouldn't betray the tremble that was spreading through my body. *What was going on here?*

He walked behind me. I heard a click and the lights went off. Just as my eyes got used to the darkness, he flashed a slide on the screen. I blinked a couple of times, then focused on the picture. It was a fat kid. I guess Principal Davis expected me to say something rotten. "Nice kid," I said. "I'll bet he listens to his mother and cleans off his plate at every meal."

There was no comment from behind me. Click-swish. The slide

changed. A baby. "Cute," I said. Click-swish. An old man. "Looks like a nice guy. Probably somebody's grandfather." Click-swish. A teacher standing in front of a blackboard. "Nice posture," I said. "And excellent handwriting."

After a couple dozen slides, curiosity won out over fear. I had to find out what would happen if I said the wrong thing. I figured it wouldn't hurt to try it once. I'd noticed that every fourth or fifth slide looked like a teacher. The next time one came up, I said, "Wow. What a dork."

A jolt shot through my arm. I tried to jerk away, but the strap held my arm down. It only lasted for an instant. Afterward, I realized the shock hadn't really hurt. Even so, I didn't like the way it felt at all.

Behind me, Principal Davis remained silent. He changed the slide. For the rest of the hour, I made sure not to say anything bad.

"Well," the principal said when he unstrapped me. "I believe we've made some progress."

"That would be a first for you, wouldn't it?" I asked. As the words left my mouth, I braced for another shock. Then I realized the strap was off.

Principal Davis glared at me, but then shifted back to that dangerous smile. "I'll see you here tomorrow," he said.

I headed for the door. And got another shock.

"By the way," Principal Davis said, "it's less than a month since you arrived, but your teachers didn't see any point in waiting, so we held your review this afternoon. It didn't take long."

"What?" I spun back toward him.

"Needless to say, you didn't pass."

"But . . ." As the memories of the day flashed through my mind, I realized there was nothing I could say. I'd run wild, and now they were getting me back. Still, it wasn't fair that they'd had the review early. "You didn't give me a chance to tell my side . . ."

"Surely you don't have any illusions about your behavior," he said. "You couldn't possibly believe you would ever be fit for a normal classroom." He turned away from me and started fiddling with the slide projector.

I went back to the third floor. I guess my legs were weak from an hour of tension. I stumbled twice on the steps. Torchie and Cheater left the room when I came in. Fine. I didn't need them.

I skipped dinner. There was no way I was going to sit there with everyone staring at me, wondering what had happened. I'm sure the whole school knew I'd been taken away by Principal Davis.

That night, I dreamed I was being dragged to the electric chair. I couldn't remember who I murdered.

The next day, I had lunch with Trash again. After class, I was escorted back to the chair. This time, I didn't get zapped. Principal Davis seemed disappointed.

The day after that, I tried to start a conversation with Trash at lunch. "So, where are you from?" I asked him. This was just wonderful. Here I was trying to get to know one of the school's biggest losers. What was I going to do next? Shine Mr. Langhorn's shoes? Take Ms. Crenshaw out for dinner and dancing? Write love poems to Miss Nomad? Maybe volunteer to help clean up the tables after lunch?

I was quickly spiraling down to the bottom of the fish tank we called Edgeview, hovering right above the gravel where all the losers waited, living in the midst of rotting food and waste products. Anyone who's ever taken a good look at a fish tank knows that the bottom is a pretty crappy place.

"West Hanover," Trash said, naming a small town about ten miles from Edgeview.

"I'm from Spencer," I told him. Great. I was having an actual conversation with someone who threw silverware for fun and tore up magazines in his spare time. Maybe he could teach me how to smash plates.

Trash didn't respond. I guess that was about as much conversation as he wanted. I wondered whether I should try again. But something happened before I had a chance to decide. As Trash reached for his fork, it flew from his tray.

He didn't throw it. He didn't smack it or flip it into the air. I swear he didn't touch it.

The fork moved by itself.

WHY I LIKE BEING ME

DOMINIC "LUCKY" CALABRIZI

Hey. What's not to like? I'm a fun guy. And I'm very generous to my friends. So they like me, too.

IN THE NAME OF SCIENCE

*T*rash's fork shot a foot in the air, then fell and hit the edge of the table. It bounced from the table and clattered to the floor. As far as I could tell, nobody paid attention to the slight tinkle the cheap piece of metal made. They were used to Trash throwing stuff.

But he hadn't thrown it. For a stunned moment, I felt like a little kid watching his first magic show. A rush of excitement hit me with the force of an ocean wave. "Telekinesis!" I shouted, leaping from my chair. I couldn't believe that I'd missed the obvious explanation for so long. *Trash was telekinetic.* He could move stuff with his mind. He might not have any control over what he was doing, but he definitely had the power.

"What'd you say?" he asked.

"I said that . . ." I stopped as images flooded back, angry faces of former friends, reminding me what had happened when I'd told Torchie, Cheater, and Flinch about their powers. Not only had they refused to believe me—they'd turned against me. Trash wasn't my friend, he was just someone I'd shared a table with for three days. But I didn't want another enemy. I didn't want to cut myself off from this last human contact. This was pathetic. I couldn't believe how low I was sinking.

"What?" he asked again.

"Nothing." I sat back down and finished my lunch. As the cafeteria cleared, I stayed in my seat and tried to make sense of everything I'd seen. My discovery of Trash's telekinesis meant there were four kids at

Edgeview with psychic powers. Torchie, Flinch, Cheater, and Trash. Were there others? Lucky was always finding things. Was he lucky, or was something more going on?

I didn't know. But I needed to find out. I grabbed a notebook and started listing all the kids I could think of who might have psychic powers. I decided that I'd write down absolutely anything I'd seen that was strange or unusual. I figured if I kept notes, I might discover some patterns. None of this would have been necessary if Cheater had cooperated.

"One experiment," I muttered, slamming my fist on the table. "One stupid experiment." That's all I needed. If they'd just agreed to that, everything would have been fine.

"What's up, Martin?"

The voice caught me by surprise. I shut the notebook and looked up at Mr. Briggs.

"What do you care? I heard you all spent a whole ten seconds deciding my fate at your last meeting."

"I would have liked to take more time. But I don't think the results would have been any different." He shook his head and laughed. "I'll say this. You've certainly made an impression at Edgeview."

"You think this is funny?"

"Sorry. No. I didn't mean to laugh. Look, we're trying to do what's best for you. Honest." Mr. Briggs walked to the other side of the table, pulled out a chair, turned it around backward, and plopped down. The knight in armor on his Rutgers T-shirt peered over the back of the chair. I'd have been happy to run him through with a lance if I'd had one.

"Did I just hear you say my favorite word?"

I stared at him. I didn't have a clue what he was talking about. Obviously, he wanted to change to subject. He didn't have the guts to talk about my review. Face-to-face, they were all cowards. Honest.

"Experiment," he said.

I didn't answer.

"Well, maybe I heard wrong." He stood up. "If you do happen to run an experiment, let me know how it goes. I'd be interested in your findings."

More than you'd believe, I thought as I watched him leave.

When he reached the hallway, he turned back and said, "Better get going or you'll be late for class. Then you'll be in big trouble." He smiled when he said that. I guess he smiled because I had his class next. I didn't return the smile. He was just making a pathetic attempt to get on my good side after stabbing me in the back.

I waited for him to get far enough ahead so he wouldn't think I was following him, then gathered my books and headed to class. As I found a spot on the carpet, Mr. Briggs went to the blackboard and said, "I want to put aside our lesson and talk about something else. How many of you know how to design and run an experiment?"

One or two kids raised their hands. Everyone else just sat there. The kids with their hands up looked around, then lowered their hands. Mr. Briggs nodded. "That's what I thought. The key to science is knowing how to design and carry out an experiment. Without that, everything else you're learning is useless. Of course, I'm sure some of you feel that it's all useless anyhow."

That got a laugh from most of the kids.

Mr. Briggs looked right at me. "Anyone want to suggest an experiment? How about you, Martin?"

I shook my head.

"Come on, Martin," he said. "Give it a try."

"No."

He shrugged. "Somebody else? Give me some ideas. What shall we investigate?"

"Nuclear bombs," Flinch shouted from the back of the room.

"Maybe next year," Mr. Briggs said after the class had stopped laughing. "Right now, we're fresh out of uranium."

Another suggestion came from behind me. This one was quieter, spoken rather than shouted, but it might as well have blared through the speakers of the world's loudest rock band as far I was concerned.

"How about mind reading?" the voice asked.

WHY I LIKE BEING ME

DENNIS WOO

Hey. What's not to like? I'm a fun guy. And I'm very generous to my friends. So they like me, too.

WHAT'S ON YOUR MIND?

I stared at Cheater, who'd just made the suggestion. For an instant, I felt hope. *Maybe he believed.* . . . Now that he'd had time to think about it, he must have realized I was right.

Cheater smirked at me and my hopes vanished. I realized this was his own private joke. I didn't think he was very funny. At least there was no way Mr. Briggs would go for something like that. A science teacher wouldn't mess around with psychic stuff.

"Excellent suggestion, Dennis," Mr. Briggs said. He strolled across the room to give Cheater a pat on the head, then returned to the board and wrote MIND READING in big letters.

Whatever Cheater's motives, this was perfect. If the whole class proved I was right, Cheater couldn't blame me.

"That's not science," Lucky said. "Let's pick something else."

"Anything can be investigated scientifically," Mr. Briggs told him. He turned back to the class. "I want each of you to try to come up with an experiment that we could use to test for mind reading."

"Is this homework?" Torchie asked.

Mr. Briggs nodded. "Sure. Let's say that's your assignment. Take a few days. We'll wait until Monday to see what everyone comes up with. To help you out, I'll tell you about some famous experiments that scientists have carried out in the past."

He spent the rest of the period talking about Newton, Galileo, and other scientists. But I had a hard time paying attention. I was thinking about what would happen when the class started running the experiments.

On the way out, I caught up with Cheater and asked, "What did you do that for?"

"Just to show you how wrong you are," he said.

"I'm not wrong. You'll see. Why can't you accept the truth? What are you scared of?"

"I'm not scared of anything," he said. But there was something in his eyes that told me he was lying. Before I could say anything else, he rushed away.

I continued my search for other kids with special powers. I saw a lot of strange stuff during the rest of the day, though most of it was just bad behavior.

But I did see a couple of things worth writing down. Lucky found two pencils, three dimes, and a candy bar—all in a single afternoon. That's just when I was watching. Who knows what else he found? He never acted surprised. It seemed like he just knew where stuff was.

By the end of the day, I had a list of seven more kids who might have some kind of psychic powers. By Friday, the list had grown to over two dozen. I had plenty of time to study my notes on Friday evening— Torchie had skipped into town with his friends. He hadn't said a word when he'd left the room.

I couldn't understand them. If someone told me I had a special ability, I'd be thrilled. It would be great to know what people were thinking, or to know what was going to happen. It would be extremely cool to move things with my mind or see the future. But there was no point daydreaming about that. I didn't have any special talents, except maybe the power to get my teachers so angry they'd strap me to a chair and shock me or slam my head against a wall. I'm sure Dad would have approved of that form of education. At least I'd finished my week of detention without further pain.

I was still awake when Torchie came back from town. I had to do something. I couldn't keep living like this. "You guys going to stay mad at me forever?" I asked.

He sat down and looked at the magazines on his desk. Then he glanced out the window. His eyes flickered in my direction once or twice, but quickly bounced away. I realized it might be as rough for him as it was for me. He was so eager to be friends with the whole world, he must hate having to be enemies with anyone. Especially someone he had to share a room with. "We aren't mad," he finally mumbled.

"Yeah, you are."

Torchie shrugged and studied his picture of Mars. "Well, maybe a little."

"Look, don't expect me to start begging."

He stared down at his sneakers. "Maybe if you knocked off all that crazy stuff about mind reading—"

"It's not crazy, it's . . ." I stopped. Did I want to be right, or did I want to have friends? It didn't seem fair that I had to choose, but that's the way it had worked out. I couldn't look somewhere else for friends. I was stuck at Edgeview. Stuck here for good now, thanks to Mr. Briggs and the other teachers. Was it really that important to prove I was right? "Can we just forget the whole thing?" I asked. I wouldn't say another word—until the experiment proved I was right.

Torchie looked at me out of the sides of his eyes. "That would be great."

I hadn't realized how tense I'd been until then. Ever since they'd gotten angry, I'd been walking around like a stretched-out rubber band. Now I could feel my whole body relax. "I'm really sorry about what I said to you."

"That's okay. I'm not mad. Honest."

I felt I had to do something special. I went to my desk and fished around in the bottom drawer until I found what I was looking for. "Here, I want you to have this."

I held out my peace offering, hoping it would make Torchie happy.

LETTER TO THE EDITOR

THE EDGEVIEW EXPRESS
DATED THE PREVIOUS MONDAY

Dear Editor,
Those who have been following the issue know that the legislature is considering a merger of the regional alternative schools. Such a move would benefit all the citizens of our town. I urge everyone to call their State representatives and let them know how we feel.

Gordon Blathwell

PICK A CARD, ANY CARD

Torchie's eyes lit up. Okay—maybe that was a bad choice of words. But I could tell he was excited. "Wow, a harmonica," he said, taking the gift. "I've always wanted one. You sure?"

"Yeah, I'm sure. My sister gave it to me last April for my birthday. I think it was her idea of a joke. I never learned to play it. I just threw it in my bag when I packed. Guess I threw it in for you." It was the perfect gift for him. As far as I could tell, it was pretty much fireproof except for the little reeds on the inside of each hole. And they tended to get pretty spitty, so they'd be safe as soon as he started playing.

"But you didn't even know me back then."

I was about to say, *Maybe I'm psychic,* but I caught myself. It wasn't a good time for that kind of joke.

Torchie blew into the harmonica, producing a batch of random notes, then pulled it away from his mouth and smiled. "Great. Did you recognize that?"

"Give me a clue."

"It was '*Oh Susannah,*' " he said.

"Right. Yeah. Now I recognize it. Good job." I got the sinking feeling I'd just created a monster.

"Too bad I can't play and sing at the same time. That would be cool."

"Yeah. Too bad."

Torchie spent the next hour or so happily making noises with the harmonica. Some of the notes even sort of resembled songs if you didn't listen too closely. At least he wasn't angry with me anymore.

The next day, at breakfast, it seemed as if an invisible signal had been sent to the other kids. Maybe it was the sight of Torchie and me standing together in line. Anyhow, Cheater and Flinch and Lucky once again recognized my existence. Except for a layer of coolness that I knew would eventually melt, everything was headed back the way it had been before.

Almost everything.

As I sat down with them, I snuck a guilty look at Trash, alone at his table. Maybe he expected me to sit with him. He glanced toward me. I thought about asking him to join us. But I'd just patched things up with the others. I didn't think it was the right time. I felt like a rat. I'd used him when I needed company, and now I was abandoning him. Maybe that should be my nickname. Martin the Rat.

As rotten as I felt about Trash, the rottenness was diluted by relief. I was back from exile.

Even though I'd decided to keep my mouth shut, I still kept my eyes open for anything unusual. But by Monday, when I went to Mr. Briggs's class, I hadn't found any new suspects to add to my list. Maybe his lecture on scientific methods had made me look at things more carefully. If you want to see something badly enough, you're going to see it even if it isn't there.

"All right, class," Mr. Briggs said once we'd all gotten comfortable. "Let's hear your ideas for experiments."

Bloodbath spoke out. "I figured I could decide to hit someone. If he stayed in the room, we'd know he didn't read my mind." He chuckled. Then he smashed one fist onto the floor.

"Very interesting," Mr. Briggs said, "but I don't know how scientific that would be."

The class discussed ideas. A couple of the kids had heard about Zenner cards, though they didn't know them by that name. I did, because of the reading I'd done. A standard set has five different symbols; a square, a star, wavy lines, and a couple of other things. There are five of each, so a deck has twenty-five cards. One person looks at a card, and the other person tries to read his mind and say what the card is or guess the card before anyone sees it.

The rest of the class leaped on the idea of the cards. Even though I knew more about the subject than anyone in the room, I kept my mouth shut. I really wanted to stay out of it. And I didn't want to give Mr. Briggs the satisfaction of thinking he'd gotten me involved.

"Okay," Mr. Briggs said when the discussion started to die down. "We all seem to like the cards, but we still need to design the experiment. How should we do it?"

"We have to switch around," Flinch said. "So we get as many combinations of kids as possible."

"Great," Mr. Briggs said. "The more pairs we test, the more data we gather. It would take a long time if we ran every possible pairing. So we can't do that. But we can run tests for a day or two and see how many we can get done. But first, we have to make the cards. I'll bring in some supplies tomorrow and we can pitch in to assemble the decks. Then we can run tests on Wednesday and Thursday. Friday, we can examine our results."

He walked back to the blackboard and picked up where he'd left off on the regular lesson. I didn't have to be a mind reader to tell that most of the kids were excited about the experiment. Cheater, who was chattering away with Flinch, seemed as excited as everyone else. I guess he was sure the test would prove he didn't have any special talents.

As it turned out, the one absolute thing the experiment proved was that I couldn't see into the future.

TESTING, TESTING . . .

*T*uesday afternoon, Mr. Briggs dumped a bagful of playing cards on the classroom floor. "Pair up. Take twenty-five cards." He passed out sheets of paper with the five symbols printed on them. I guess he'd designed the pages on the computer. He also passed out glue and those blunt scissors—the kind people give little kids so they won't hurt themselves or someone else. "Get to work," he said.

We started making the decks, gluing the symbols onto the faces of the playing cards. There was a square, a star, a plus sign, a minus sign, and wavy lines.

"Why can't we just use the pieces of paper?" Torchie asked.

"Anyone?" Mr. Briggs asked the class.

"The backs have to be identical," Flinch said.

"Right." Mr. Briggs nodded. "If there are any differences in the shape of the cards, the test results aren't valid."

We made up all the cards we needed by the end of class. The next day, we started the tests. Before we began, Mr. Briggs gave us some instructions. "The tester has to keep score. Get out a piece of paper. Every time the subject makes a guess, write either H for a hit or M for a miss, but don't let the other person see the card, even after he's guessed. That information could be used to help make the next guess. When you finish the test, count up the hits and misses. I wrote a program to keep track of the scores. Go to the computer, select the name of the sender and receiver, and enter how many hits you recorded." He paused for a moment. I guess he was waiting to see if there were questions. Nobody said anything. "Okay, pair up and let's get started."

For the first test, I was paired with Lucky. I got six right. Lucky got five right—that was about what I expected. There were five different symbols, so each guess had one chance in five of being right. With twenty-five cards, a person who was just guessing blindly would be right about five times. A person might beat the odds and guess right six or seven times—maybe even eight—but only someone who could read minds would get a high score like fifteen or twenty.

"Pick another partner," Mr. Briggs said after everyone had finished the first pair of experiments.

I found myself with one of the runts. I got five hits. So did he. Right on the average for each of us. On the last round of the day, as everyone scrambled for partners, I took too long making up my mind. There was only one person left. Cheater looked at me from across the room. I'd avoided him so far. I just didn't want to be part of the proof. That way, he couldn't blame me. But now I had no choice.

"I'll go first," he said. "You be the tester." He seemed happy we were working together and eager to get started.

I reached for the top card. It took me two tries to get a grip on it. I stared at the figure on the face of the card. *Square,* I thought, trying to imagine a giant square.

"Star," Cheater guessed.

I wrote *M* on the pad to record the miss and picked up the next card. It was a cross.

"Wavy lines," Cheater guessed.

That's how it went. As each card slid off the deck, I felt a little more of my confidence drain away. Cheater missed every single one. At first I was disappointed. But as I entered the score in the computer, I felt a bit relieved, too. Maybe it all had been my imagination. Maybe it was time to forget the whole thing.

I got seven right when Cheater tested me. "Hey, it looks like you're the mind reader," he said, grinning.

I held back a nasty reply. He was just trying to be friendly.

That was the last test we had time for that period. We ran another three sets on Thursday. By then, everyone was talking about the experiment.

"I got eight, once," Torchie said. "But another time, I just got three."

"It balances out," I told him. "If you ran one test, just about anything could happen. One test doesn't mean much at all. If you ran ten tests, you'd probably come close to the average. But if you ran a thousand tests, you'd get even closer." I wanted to explain more about averages, but I stopped when I noticed his eyes start to glaze over.

My own words lingered in my mind. *One test doesn't mean much at all.* I wondered whether my one test with Cheater was a fluke. Maybe he'd scored higher with other people. I'd find out soon enough.

The next day, everyone seemed eager to hear the results. "Well, class," Mr. Briggs said, "we have some interesting numbers." He had the computer keyboard in his lap. "First, let's see if anyone scored higher than we expected, since that's the whole point of our investigation. I'll pull up a list of subjects who averaged better than five hits on their tests."

We all crowded around the monitor. A bunch of names scrolled up. I could feel a wave of excitement pass through the room. Nobody—except for me—had ever expected any sort of special results. And I definitely hadn't expected more than one mind reader to show up in the class.

"Now let's check the specific details," Mr. Briggs said. He hit a few more keys. The screen changed. "We seem to have two groups that had high scores. Robert, Justin, and Trevor all did better than average. I'll put up their results and see what you think."

I looked at the information. Each of the three had scored a perfect round of twenty-five hits. That was amazing. Then I noticed something else. Each had only done it once. And in every case, the tester was the same—Avery Morrison, one of the runts.

"Squinty," a couple of kids said, calling Avery by his nickname. They'd realized the pattern at the same time I did.

Everyone turned toward him. Squinty looked back, peering at us through his thick glasses. "What's everyone staring at?"

Mr. Briggs handed him a deck of the test cards. "Hold one up, but don't let me see."

Avery held up a card, raising it close to his face. "No, not here," Mr. Briggs said. "Let's go over to where you usually sit. The light's better over there." He followed Squinty to a corner of the rug near a window. After they sat down, Mr. Briggs tilted his head a bit, as if searching for something, and then said, "Minus sign."

"Yeah," Squinty said. "You got it."

"Square," Mr. Briggs said for the second card.

"Wow. Right again," Squinty told him.

"Another square."

"Yup."

"Star."

"Holy smokes. You got another one."

Mr. Briggs named a couple more cards before Squinty caught on. By then, the rest of us were laughing hard enough to split a gut. It was like watching a magic act. Robert, Justin, and Trevor, who each had done the same thing during the actual test, were laughing the hardest of all.

Finally, Mr. Briggs, who was laughing, too, said, "This is a great lesson. It shows one way an experiment can go wrong. In this case, nobody intended to cheat, but I suspect that the opportunity was just irresistible to the three of you who noticed the reflection in Avery's glasses. Of course, the instant we saw perfect scores, we should have become suspicious."

As Mr. Briggs said this, I heard Bloodbath say, "Damn." Then Bloodbath started looking around like he was thinking about leaving the room.

Mr. Briggs, staring at Bloodbath, said, "So someone who wanted to be *really* clever while cheating shouldn't get perfect scores. It would be a lot better to miss a couple of times." He went back to the computer and pulled up some more information. He didn't say anything about the data—he just pointed to a column of numbers on the screen.

I think everyone understood what was going on right away. Bloodbath had gotten four perfect scores. But the tester in each case had been one of his buddies. They'd obviously cheated just for the sake of cheating. Maybe they thought it was a good joke. Maybe they were so used to cheating whenever they could that they'd just naturally done it during the test. But, as Mr. Briggs had pointed out, they hadn't been clever enough.

"Now let's throw out these cases and look at the rest of our results. Let's see who did better than five right." He tapped a few more keys. "As you can see, nobody managed to score six hits per test. The highest average was five-point-seven-six—roughly five and three-quarters. So, at least as far as this experiment is concerned, we have no real evidence of psychic ability."

That was it, then. Scientific proof that I had been wrong.

I heard Cheater snicker. When he caught me looking at him, he said, "Sorry." I guess he hadn't meant to laugh at me. That was okay. I sort of deserved it.

"As a matter of fact," Mr. Briggs said, "the average for the entire class, once we throw out the bad data, is just a bit better than four and a half hits. I suspect it would be a lot closer to five if we ran more tests. But we've done enough to learn a few things. And that, my friends, should always be the point of one of these exercises."

The class spent the rest of the period discussing the test and the results. Mr. Briggs talked about ways to design a better experiment, and ways to prevent cheating. Apparently, that was a big problem. Sometimes people wanted to prove something so badly that they cheated when they ran a test.

In a way, I was relieved that we'd run an actual scientific test and it had shown no evidence that anyone could read minds. I could get on with my life and stop driving myself crazy with wild ideas about that kind of stuff. As I left class, I shook my head, thinking about how stupid Bloodbath had been when he'd tried to get away with those perfect scores. It was funny how he'd given himself away by cheating too successfully. But that led me to another thought. It came to me so suddenly that I wanted to dash right back into the room.

Instead, I waited until Mr. Briggs left. The program was still up on the computer. Even better, the file with the results was open. I pulled down the menu and sent the data to the printer. It was the old kind that makes a lot of noise and spits out a single line at a time. I watched the pages as they inched out, revealing something I'd almost missed. My hand shook so badly I ripped the edge of the last sheet as I tore it from the printer.

There was no doubt about it. No mistake. I had definite proof. I wasn't sure if I wanted it, but I had it.

The question was: What should I do with it?

Subject Trial #	Martin Tester	Score	Percentage
1	Dominic	6	24
2	Jonas	5	20
3	Dennis	7	28
4	Tyler	5	12
5	Waylon	3	20
6	Andrew	5	20
	Average	5.16	20.66

Subject Trial #	Dominic Tester	Score	Percentage
1	Martin	5	20
2	Tyler	4	16
3	Eddie	4	16
4	Willis	5	20
5	Philip	6	24
6	Dennis	5	20
	Average	4.83	19.33

Subject Trial #	Dennis Tester	Score	Percentage
1	Eddie	0	0
2	Willis	0	0
3	Martin	0	0
4	Andrew	0	0
5	Robert	0	0
6	Dominic	0	0
	Average	0	0

NOTHING BUT THE PROOF

The smart thing would have been to just forget what I knew. There was no way they'd want to hear this. But, if I'd been good at doing the smart thing, I wouldn't have ended up at Edgeview.

I waited until that evening, when Flinch, Lucky, and Cheater were in the room with Torchie and me. Then I waited until they started talking about science class. That didn't take long.

"You know," Cheater said, "I'd bet that Mr. Briggs could get fired for that experiment."

"You're crazy," Torchie said.

"No, he's right," Lucky said. "Any of that kind of different stuff, they get real funny about it. In my last school, this teacher explained some things to us about witches. It wasn't bad stuff, just how some people had certain beliefs. She didn't swallow any of it herself—none of us did. She just told us about it. And she got fired."

"Exactly," Cheater said. "Mr. Briggs could get in big trouble."

"But it was worth it," I said.

They all turned toward me. I pulled the printout from my notebook and scanned it again to boost my courage. Now that I'd started, I had to convince them. If I failed, they'd probably hate me forever.

"Think about this," I said. "What would your score be if you answered the same thing each time? What if for each of the twenty-five guesses you said 'square'?" Suddenly, I had a very good idea how a parachutist felt the first time he jumped out of a plane. I could almost feel myself hurtling through the air. My stomach sure seemed to believe I was plunging toward a canyon filled with jagged rocks. I waited for my parachute to open.

"But there aren't twenty-five squares," Torchie said.

"Right," Flinch said. "There are five. So you'd score five out of twenty-five. That's one out of five, or twenty percent. You'd be right at the average."

I took a deep breath. *Here it comes.* This was the leap of thinking I had to help them make. It was obvious to me, but I was good at math. So was Flinch. Cheater was, too, but I knew he wouldn't do anything to help me. Torchie might have trouble following the explanation. But if I could convince the others, he'd go along with them.

"Now," I said, looking at Cheater, "is there any way to make sure you'd get a lower score? Can you think of anything you could do to make sure you'd only get four right, or three, or two?"

"You could . . ." Torchie started to say. Then I guess he stopped to think. Cheater remained silent. So did Lucky.

"Can't be done," Flinch said. "There's no way to average less than five hits in the long run. Whether you just said 'square' each time, or if you mixed them up, you'd still hit one out of five, in the long run, no matter what."

"So," I said, not taking my eyes from Cheater, "how could someone miss every card, not just in one test, but six times in a row?"

"That's impossible," Flinch said. "You'd have to get some of them right just by chance."

As Flinch spoke, Cheater looked away from me.

"Unless you knew what the right answer was," I said. "If you knew the right answer, but you wanted to prove you didn't, it would be easy to get every answer wrong. Easy, but not a good way to hide your ability. Mr. Briggs was interested in kids who got more than five right. He didn't bother to look at the other side—*kids who got less than five.*" I held up the printout and pointed at Cheater's scores.

"Wow. You're right," Flinch said, grabbing the printout from my hand. "It would be impossible to miss every one, unless you knew what the right answers were. Maybe—just maybe—you could miss all the cards on one test. But on *every* test? Give me a break."

Even Torchie saw that I was right. "Cheater, you *can* read minds."

Cheater shook his head. "No, I can't. Mr. Briggs didn't say anything. He would have said something . . ."

"Mr. Briggs was looking for hits, not misses," I said. "You should be glad he was. If he'd noticed your score, he'd have known right away that something was wrong."

"But . . ." Cheater looked around the room. "Lucky, you don't believe this nonsense, do you?"

Lucky just shrugged.

"Flinch," Cheater said, "you can't swallow this stuff?"

"It makes perfect sense to me," Flinch said. "Numbers don't lie."

Cheater turned to Torchie. "Come on, Torchie," he said, "at least you believe me. I can't read minds, and even if I could, I'd never tell anyone about your secret hiding place."

Torchie gasped. "How'd you know? That's just what I was thinking." He stared at Cheater for a moment, then looked around at the rest of us. "I was worried that Cheater would read my mind and know where I hid my favorite comics."

I could see it in their faces. They believed. Torchie was sure now—there was no doubt in his face, just wonder and amazement. The same with Lucky and Flinch.

I watched Cheater. I expected him to be angry or happy. Instead, he looked like he was about to cry. "I don't want to be different," he said quietly.

"But you are," I told him. "Hey, everyone is different in some way, right?"

"Not this different," Cheater said.

"No choice," Flinch told him. "You are what you are. You gotta live with it."

"There's this guy in my town," Cheater said. "Everyone called him Crazy Wally. He walked around talking to himself. He heard voices. People laughed at him. Kids teased him. One day, the voices told him to get even. He killed three people before the police shot him." Cheater stared right at me. "I'm not crazy."

"Hey, nobody said you were." I began to understand his anger and fear. "You don't hear voices. You aren't walking around talking to yourself. That's not what it's like, is it?"

Cheater shook his head. He started to speak again, but it took several tries. "I didn't want to believe it." He looked down at the floor.

We all waited quietly. Finally, he went on. "Sometimes, I guess I just know stuff. It's not like I hear it. I can't pick through people's brains. I guess I only get what someone is actually thinking. It's like their thoughts show up in my mind."

"Like a memory?" I asked.

"Yeah, that's it," Cheater said. "But I know stuff on my own, too. I'm really smart. Ask me anything. Anything at all."

"Hey, relax. We know you're smart," I told him. "You're probably the smartest kid I've ever met."

Cheater smacked his leg with his fist. "But sometimes I can't tell it apart—the stuff I learned and the stuff that pops up."

"So you're not even sure where it's coming from," I said. That explained his problems in school. "When you're taking a test, you think the ideas are from your own mind. You don't hear the thoughts of the kid next to you—the thoughts are just there in your mind."

"Yeah. I guess . . ."

Flinch started to laugh.

"What's so funny?" Cheater asked.

"All your life, you've never cheated, right?" Flinch asked.

Cheater nodded. "Never. Not until the experiment."

"So after all that, after a whole lifetime of being honest, when you finally decide to cheat you're so bad at it you get caught right away." Flinch rolled on the floor, laughing so hard he started to gasp for breath.

Cheater laughed, too. Then his face grew serious and he looked around the room. "I don't try to spy on anyone. I really can't."

"We know," Lucky said. He put a hand on Cheater's shoulder. "I trust you."

"Hey, don't worry," Torchie said. "We aren't afraid of you or nothing. Honest."

"You aren't crazy. And you aren't the only one with special powers," I said.

They all turned back to me. I felt like I was jumping out of another plane.

"You aren't going to start that again, are you?" Torchie asked.

"No," I said, "I'll just sit here and let you set your chair on fire." I pointed toward his left hand.

"Youch!" Torchie jumped up from his seat. On the arm of the chair, where he'd rested his fingers against the wood, a smoldering spot gave off a small wisp of smoke. "Who did that?"

"You did, Torchie," I said. "Somehow, you can start fires. There's no other explanation."

Torchie stepped away from his chair as the glowing area dimmed and then vanished, leaving a charred blotch. He didn't say anything. I turned toward Flinch. "What do I have to do? Throw stuff at you? Come on, Flinch, this is the time. Cheater has stopped lying to himself. So has Torchie. Well? As you just said, you gotta learn to live with it."

"You're right. And I guess I gotta talk about it. Stuff speeds up sometimes," Flinch said. "I see something about to hit me, so I jump out of the way. Then everything slows down until the world catches up. But I've already gotten out of the way. That's how it's been my whole life. I figured it was kind of like that for everyone. Or else I was some kind of freak."

"You're seeing into the future," I told him. "Not very far, but definitely into the future. That's why you always have the flipper ready in time when you play pinball."

"No, that can't be it. I'm . . . ." Flinch stopped. He couldn't seem to think up another explanation.

"And you have a talent for finding things," I told Lucky. "I'm not sure what it means. Maybe you sense the objects. Or maybe you sense some sort of mark left on the object by the owner. I don't know. But it sure isn't a skill everyone has."

Lucky shrugged. "I've always figured I was just lucky."

"You are," I said. "You all are." As much as I should have been thrilled that they finally believed me, there was a sad side I couldn't ignore. I guess I felt left out. They had these wonderful abilities. I had nothing. But at least I could help one more person—someone I'd treated pretty rottenly. "There are others," I said.

"Who?" Lucky asked.

"Well, I'm not positive in some of the cases, but there's one person I'm absolutely sure about. Hang on, I'll go get him." I went down the hall and knocked on Trash's door.

"What?" he asked when I stepped inside.

"There are some kids down the hall who want to meet you," I said.

"Is this your idea of a joke?" he asked.

"No joke," I said. "Promise."

"Why would they want to meet me?" he asked.

"Let's just say you have a lot in common." I turned toward the door, then stopped. "Well?"

Trash shrugged and got up. I could understand that he'd want to be cautious. But as he crossed the room, I thought I saw the slightest hint of a smile on his lips.

UNFINISHED LETTER FROM DOROTHY ANDERSON

Dear Martin,

I'm sorry I didn't write sooner. The house feels different without you here. Everyone misses you. Especially your sister. Your father misses you too, of course

PART THREE

POWERS

NOW WHAT?

The others accepted Trash pretty quickly. I guess it wasn't hard for them to realize they shared a rare and common bond—especially Torchie and Trash. Since the two of them had the most destructive powers, they'd gotten into the most trouble. For the first week, I had to walk down the hall and invite Trash to our room each evening.

"Hey, why don't you come over and hang out with us?"

"You sure?"

"Yeah, come on."

But then he started popping in by himself. I guess it had been a long time since anyone had welcomed him anywhere. I knew what that felt like.

Trash certainly added some excitement to our lives. We were never sure when he'd launch a book across the room or tip a chair, dumping out whoever was sitting in it. I learned to keep an eye on Flinch. As soon has he ducked, I knew it was time to hug the carpet and cover my head.

The word we heard the most from Trash was, "Sorry."

I finally told him to knock it off. It was Friday, but we'd decided not to sneak out of the school. We didn't want to ditch Trash, but we didn't think the town of Edgeview was ready for a visit from him. Besides, one of those bitter-cold mid-February storms had made the trip less appealing than usual.

So we were hanging out in the room. Torchie was playing the harmonica. All of a sudden, his chair jolted as if someone had given it a hard kick. It didn't move far enough to knock him off, but it sure got his attention. "Whoa!" Torchie shouted as jumped from his seat.

"Sorry," Trash said.

"No big deal," Torchie told him. He sat back down and returned to the thirty-ninth chorus of "Red River Valley."

A minute later, Cheater screamed and leaped from the floor where he'd been sitting. As he twisted around, I saw the back of his underwear hanging over the top of his jeans.

"Wow," I said, amazed at the sight. "That's got to be the world's biggest wedgie."

"Sorry," Trash said.

"Did you do that to him on purpose?" Lucky asked as Cheater straightened out his clothing.

"No way," Trash said. "I'd never touch anybody's underwear on purpose. Not even with my mind." He shuddered.

"Yeah," Flinch said. "If you did that, you'd need to get brainwashed."

Before I could laugh, a pencil flew from my desk and plunked against the side of my head just hard enough to make me say, "Ouch."

"Sorry." Trash picked up the pencil and put it back on the desk.

"How about you just say sorry once a day?" I suggested. "Say it in the morning, and that'll cover whatever happens during the next twenty-four hours. Okay?"

"I'll try." He dropped his gaze to the floor for a moment, but then looked back up. He reminded me of a puppy who'd just been scolded.

I glanced around the room. "Everyone happy with that?"

"Sure," Torchie said. "Fine with me."

The others nodded.

"And you," I said, staring at Flinch. "Stop it with the sneezing thing. Someone is going to figure out what's happening. You did it again this afternoon in science."

Flinch had fallen into a habit of saying "Gesundheit" right before any of us sneezed. That afternoon, he'd even handed me a tissue. He must have been keeping it ready, just waiting for an opportunity. He'd reached over and thrust it into my hand during class and whispered, "Bless you." A half second later, I'd sneezed. It's a good thing Mr. Briggs hadn't been looking.

"You have to knock it off," I said.

Flinch grinned and, doing a great imitation of Trash, he hung down his head and said, "I'm sorry."

"It's not funny," Cheater said. "If they find out about us, bad things are gonna happen. People hate anyone who's different."

"Yeah. They could cut us up to figure out how we work," Lucky said.

"That's"—I almost said *crazy*, but I caught myself in time—"not going to happen."

"Or lock us in a room," Cheater said. "You know, use us for weapons. Or as spies." He walked over and blew out a small fire that had started smoldering in the wastebasket.

"They wouldn't do that," Torchie said. "But we'd probably get split up if they found out."

"It's like a secret weapon," Lucky said. "It works best if nobody knows about it. We can't tell anyone."

"It'll work even better if you learn to control it," I said. As those words left my lips, Torchie's pillow shot across the room and whizzed past Flinch's head. Naturally, he'd dodged aside a second earlier.

"Sor—" Trash started to say. "Oops."

"How can we control it?" Torchie asked.

Trash shook his head. "I can't. I've tried."

"Me, too," Cheater said.

"There has to be something we can do." Torchie looked at me as if I had all the answers in the world.

So did the others.

Hey Marty,

Thanks for the hair clip. And it's not even my birthday. Thanks for the ticket, too. That brought back memories. Dad's angry at Mom for something. Not sure what. I think he's angry with me, too, but it's hard to tell. I sure haven't done anything wrong.

Guess what? I was flipping the dial and I caught a bunch of people way up on channel six billion, or somewhere around there, arguing about your school. I don't know what they were all concerned about. It was too boring to leave on, so I switched to that show where they talk about lawn mowing. But I figured you'd be happy to hear you were sorta on television.

Your spectacular sister,

Teri

P.S. I made lasagna last night. Is it supposed to be crunchy?

BURNING QUESTIONS

The truth is, I'd been thinking about this a lot. And I had plenty of ideas. But how could I tell them what to do when I didn't even know what it was like to have special powers? That would be like a cat trying to teach a dog to bark. Besides, Cheater and Flinch were both a lot smarter than I was. One of them should be in charge.

"Come on," Flinch said. "You've got to have some ideas."

I shook my head.

"Please, Martin," Torchie said.

Why was it so hard to say *no* to him? "Okay. I guess I have a couple of ideas." Maybe if I helped Torchie a little, someone else would take over and I could step aside. "We better start with you."

"How come?" he asked.

"Well, if Cheater reads a mind or Flinch sees what's about to happen, it's no big deal. Lucky isn't doing any harm to anyone. Trash could hurt someone, I guess. But Trash mostly throws small stuff. Right?"

"Right," Torchie said.

"But you can burn this place to the ground," I told him. "So I figure you need control more than anyone."

Torchie shrugged. "I guess."

"So we're not going to do anything for the rest of us?" Cheater asked.

"Sure," I said. "We'll work with everyone. But your problem isn't that hard. Someone will come up with something. I'd bet there's an easy solution."

"No, there isn't," Cheater said. "If there was, I'd have figured . . ." He paused and a smile spread across his face. "I get it."

Obviously, Cheater had plucked the idea as it ran through my mind. It was kind of spooky knowing my thoughts could end up inside his head. There were things in my mind I'd never want anyone to know. But he still didn't know it had come from me.

"Get what?" Flinch asked, looking in my direction.

"Yeah, Martin," Torchie said. "Tell us."

"It's no great idea or anything. Now that Cheater realizes he might be tapping into other people's thoughts, all he has to do for tests is to use different words," I explained. "Suppose he's taking a history test, and the answer he wants to write is: *General Sherman led his troops on a March through Georgia.* The trick is to change it around a bit. He can write: *Under his command, General Sherman's troops marched through Georgia,* or something like that. Just so he doesn't use exactly the same words as the kids around him." I was sure that would work. Cheater knew so much that he wouldn't have any trouble finding different ways to write test answers.

"Yeah," Flinch said. "That's a great idea. I wish you had some easy answers for me."

I'd been thinking about that, too. But I'd already gotten enough attention. I kept silent.

"Well, someone in this room has an answer," Cheater said.

It looked like there weren't going to be any secrets with this group. I figured I might as well tell Flinch my idea. "I have an answer, but it'll take some work." I leaped across the room and threw a punch at Flinch's face.

He ducked before I even had my fist halfway out. My hand shot through the air where his head had been. I had to put out my other hand to keep from smacking face-first into the wall.

"Hey, what was that for?" Flinch shouted.

"Practice," I told him. "You need to learn to hold back a bit. Try not to jump so soon this time."

"Good thinking," Flinch said. "Come on, let's try it again."

I threw another punch. Flinch waited too long. Before I could stop myself, my fist connected with his jaw. A sharp jolt shot through my wrist.

"Oh man," I said as he went down. "Are you okay?"

Flinch shook his head hard, then staggered back to his feet. "Yeah." He rubbed his jaw. "I guess sooner would have been better."

"I'm sorry. Did I hurt you?" My whole hand was starting to ache.

"Not really," Flinch said. "It's just that I've never been punched in the face before. I can't say that I like it."

"Never?" I asked.

"Never," he said. "I always managed to get out of the way. Come on. Let's try it again."

"You sure?"

He nodded.

I threw another punch. Flinch dodged too soon, but not as soon as he usually did.

"Better," I said.

"Can I hit him next?" Cheater asked. He swung his hand in a karate chop.

"I thought you didn't know any of that stuff," I said.

"I don't," Cheater said, "but it looks like fun."

Flinch glared at Cheater.

"Hang on," I said. "Everyone will get plenty of time punching Flinch. Right now, let's work with Torchie. Okay?"

They nodded.

"We need something that can put out fires," I said.

"No problem." Lucky dashed out of the room. I figured he was going to dig through the loot in his closet. Sure enough, when he came back he handed me a small blue plastic squirt gun. It was the old-fashioned kind with a squeeze trigger—not the kind that gets pumped up. A drop of water hanging off the plug in the back showed me he'd just filled the gun.

"Now what?" Torchie asked.

I tossed the water pistol to Flinch. Then I tore a piece of paper from my notebook and passed it to Torchie. "See if you can start a fire. Try to pay attention to anything happening in your mind. Once you figure out how you do it, then maybe you can get some control." I looked over at Flinch. "Your job is to make sure he doesn't get burned."

"Got it." Flinch nodded.

We all watched the piece of paper in Torchie's hand.

Suddenly, Flinch said, "Look out!" and squirted the paper.

"Hey!" Torchie shouted. "Why'd you do that?" As he spoke, a bit of steam rose from the damp paper.

"This isn't going to work," I said to Flinch. "You're reacting before it happens. Let someone else do it."

"But I could use this for practice," Flinch said. "It beats getting punched in the face. I can try to wait until the flame really starts."

"Yeah, but it doesn't beat getting burned fingers," Torchie said. "If you wait too long, I'll get hurt."

"You won't get burned," Flinch told him.

"You're right, I won't," Torchie said. "Because you aren't going to be the one with the squirt gun."

"Hold it," I shouted. "Stop arguing. Cheater, you take the water pistol. Everyone else, watch the paper and see if you notice anything. We won't get anything done if everyone is fighting."

"Yes, Dad," Flinch joked.

Oh man. He was right. I'd sounded like a parent shouting at a couple of kids who were horsing around in the back seat of a car. That's the last thing I wanted. I kept my mouth shut and concentrated on watching the paper in Torchie's hand.

Torchie managed to start a couple more fires, but he didn't seem to have any idea how he was doing it. "Enough," he said after half an hour. He slumped back in his chair.

"You know, I'll bet there are lots of people out there with special powers," Flinch said.

"Maybe," I said, "but don't go wild and start thinking every coincidence is an example of psychic powers. It has to be rare, or we'd know a lot more about it." I thought about the two dozen names on my list. One by one, I'd crossed off everyone except Lucky.

"I'm sure my grandfather was psychic," Torchie said.

Flinch laughed. "Yeah. Right. What did he do, carry a bucket of water whenever he knew you were coming?"

"No, really," Torchie said. "He had a special talent. Anytime I got hurt, he seemed to know where—even if I didn't tell him about it. If I got a shot, he patted me on the shoulder. If I had a sunburn, he slapped me on the back. He wasn't trying to hurt me. He just had a knack for finding my sore spots."

Suddenly, everyone could think of examples of friends or relatives who might have had psychic powers. I let them talk for a while, but then got back to work trying to control our group's powers.

As for Lucky, that seemed simple enough. "Just don't pick up stuff like wallets and jewelry," I said. "Then you won't be accused of stealing."

"Yeah, that'll work," he said, but something in his voice worried me. Well, unless he wanted to tell me more, there was nothing I could do.

Meanwhile, there was plenty to keep me busy. I made up some tests so Cheater could practice rephrasing his answers while we all sat around him.

Every once in a while, no matter what we were doing, I threw a punch at Flinch. Cheater was right—it was fun.

And then there was Trash. Trash was amazing.

Psi: Short term popularly used to describe various psychic phenomena.

Empath: One who actually experiences or intimately understands the feelings of others.

Synergy: The power of a group to achieve an effect greater than they could achieve as individuals.

WHY I LIKE BEING ME

WILLIS "FLINCH" DOBBS

I like being me because I'm not just good at one thing but excel in a wide range of activities. I'm a talented athlete, but I also have a sharp mind. It might seem like I'm frequently distracted and inattentive, but I'm always thinking. My mind is, if anything, not unoccupied but preoccupied. I especially enjoy thinking up jokes. As mundane as that might seem, jokes make people laugh and feel good. You could say I have a gift for comedy. And if dodge ball ever becomes an Olympic sport, I'll be going for the gold.

TRAINING TRASH

*H*is real name was Eddie, but we were all used to calling him Trash. He didn't seem to mind. Trash had said he couldn't stop stuff from flying around. "Don't try to stop it," I told him. "Try to do it."

He caught on right away. If he could intentionally use his power, he'd have a chance of controlling it. So that's what he worked on.

I was amazed that he'd never figured out the part he'd played in smashing and crashing objects. But I guess that's how it was. Long ago, he'd realized that things went flying when he was around. But until now, he'd never been able to accept that he was the cause. As soon as Trash started exercising his power, he began to have fewer unplanned incidents.

Everyone kept an eye out for other signs of talents. But we didn't see anything. So, for the moment, there were five of them. I mean, there were six of us, but only five were special. They'd started calling themselves the Psi Five, which rhymes with *high five*. Anytime they passed each other in the hall, they'd slap hands in a high five and mouth the words *Psi Five*. The first time I saw them do that, I got this funny feeling in my gut, like when I was four years old and watched the kid next door unwrap a real nice birthday present. I guess they couldn't call themselves the Psychic Six, since I didn't count. Sometimes, they called me Coach as sort of a joke since I was helping them to train. It wasn't like a real nickname, but I liked it.

And there were lots of signs of progress.

"Look," Cheater said one afternoon at the end of history class. He held up his test—he'd gotten an A. "You were right, Coach. I made sure to use my own words. It worked. It really did."

"Great." I was happy for him. He'd do fine. Though the sad part was that, in a way, it didn't really matter. Once you got dumped at Edgeview, everyone assumed you'd never get better. We were all treated as if we were incurably sick.

"Good job," Flinch said to Cheater. "You know what? It helps, understanding what's going on. It's hard work, but I'm getting better control."

It was hard work for me as well as Flinch. I must have thrown about a thousand punches a day at him. Okay, maybe not that many. But it sure felt like it. After the first day, my shoulder hurt. I didn't nail him in the jaw again, but I came frighteningly close a couple of times. Still, Flinch was learning to handle his reactions. He'd figured out this system where the faster he saw something happening, the longer he knew he had to wait before reacting.

Cheater liked to work with Flinch, too. Despite his protests about stereotyping, he loved to scream "Hiyaaaa!" and throw what I guess was some kind of karate chop.

Torchie was making progress, too. Even though he still hadn't figured out exactly what made it happen, the very fact that he spent time each day trying to start fires seemed to have cut down on unintentional flames.

I, on the other hand, managed to get into more trouble than ever. I tried—I really tried to keep my mouth shut around my teachers. But I just couldn't help it—especially when someone like Parsons got in my face and gave me a hard time. He really hated me. So did almost all the teachers.

And that explains how I was the first in our group to learn the news. Flinch could see into the future, and Cheater could read minds. Lucky could find things. But I found out what was happening the old-fashioned way. I stuck my nose where it didn't belong.

Memo From: Principal Davis
To: All Staff
Subject: Clutter

I have recently been dismayed to notice a
tendency among staff members to amass a great
quantity of clutter. It is important that we
keep all files organized and current. As I
have mentioned in several previous memos, it
is important to keep control of paperwork. I
trust I can count on all of you to cooperate
on this issue.

MOB VIOLENCE

The next Friday, right after classes. I was sitting in detention once again. It was Miss Nomad's turn to play zookeeper. But she wasn't paying much attention to us. Her desk was covered with leaning towers of papers and file folders. She was busy cleaning out one of her desk drawers when she knocked over a file folder, spilling a stack of papers.

"I got it," I said.

"Thank you, Martin." She smiled at me, and then went back to sorting through the drawer.

I guess I still felt sort of bad about some of the things I'd said to her. Maybe I could say something nice about one of her poems. I walked over to the front of her desk and started gathering up the papers. But it wasn't a pile of poems. The folder was labeled ALTERNATIVE EDUCATION COMMITTEE. When I saw that the sheet on top was a memo from Principal Davis, I couldn't help reading it. I skimmed the memo, and then the next piece of paper. It was a copy of a letter from the state Board of Education. There was a bunch of other stuff: memos, letters, even some copies of newspaper articles. I didn't look at all of it, but I saw enough to know what was going on.

After detention, I rushed upstairs. I reached the room at the same time as Cheater.

"Wait till you hear my news," he said.

"I've got news, too," I told him.

"What is it?" Torchie asked.

"The state might close this place," I explained. "They're having this big inspection at the end of the year."

"Why would they close Edgeview?" Torchie asked.

"I guess some people don't think the school is doing any good." It felt strange to realize that there were people arguing over what was best for me—people who had never met me, people who had never bothered to ask my opinion.

"Well, it isn't, is it?" Lucky said.

"I don't know." I wasn't sure. Not that it mattered what I thought. There wasn't anything any of us could do. We didn't have that kind of power. The adults were going to make the decision. And June was far away. "What's your news?" I asked Cheater.

"Check this out," he said, pulling a crumpled piece of paper from his pocket. "It was in yesterday's newspaper."

"Pinball tournament!" I said, reading the ad. "Hey, it's tonight at nine."

"So what?" Trash asked. "They won't let us go." He looked around the room at us. "Hey, what are you all grinning about?"

"You'll see," I told him. "I just hope you aren't afraid of high places." It was time for a road trip. And so we added Trash to our Friday night gang and headed off that evening for MondoVideo, our pockets filled with quarters thanks to Lucky and his endless supply.

The Edgies never had a chance.

I thought for sure Flinch would win the tournament. I hadn't counted on Trash's telekinesis. He kept giving the ball a little nudge here and there. Just enough to keep it in play and make it hit the highest-scoring targets and bumpers.

In the end, Trash took first place, Flinch took second, and I took third. I figured my third place was just as good as a first, since I was the only player without any special advantage. We all got little plastic trophies, and some angry looks from the Edgies.

I didn't think it would go any further than that. But they were waiting for us outside the arcade. Ten or twelve of them. "Get out of here," the Edgie at the front of the pack said. He looked like he was at least sixteen. He was wearing a varsity jacket—the kind you get when you play sports, with a big *E* for "Edgeview High" in front that had a picture of a football in the middle of the letter. He was the biggest one in the crowd.

"We're going," I said. I started to cross the street.

"Yeah," Flinch said. "No reason to stay. We got our trophies."

The guy with the varsity jacket swore and said, "Don't come back."

The others followed me across the street and we headed toward the school.

As we reached the wooded hill that led to the pipe, Cheater said, "Uh-oh."

"What's wrong?" I asked.

"Is anyone here thinking about kicking the crap out of me?" he asked.

"Not me," I said.

"Me either," Lucky said.

"Maybe tomorrow," Flinch told him. "But not at the moment."

"I sure ain't," Torchie said.

I had a sudden bad feeling. "Do you only pick up stuff from people real close by?" I asked Cheater.

"As far as I know," he said.

"What if a bunch of people had the same thought? You think it might carry farther?" As I said this, I looked behind us.

Half a block away, we were being stalked by a mob of Edgies.

"Should we make a run for it?" Cheater asked, glancing toward the woods.

That didn't sound like a bad idea to me. The end of the pipe was masked by bushes. If we headed right into the woods, we could be out of sight before the Edgies caught up. On the other hand, I hated to run away. I waited to see what the others did.

"I don't know about you guys," Lucky said, "but I'm tired of every-one treating me like garbage." He stopped walking and turned to face the Edgies. "Nobody's pushing me around."

"Yeah, no more," Flinch said. He stopped walking, too.

"No more," Cheater said.

Torchie nodded. He moved next to Cheater. So did I.

The varsity jacket guy stepped out from the mob as the rest of them stopped about ten feet from us. "I don't want to see you around here again. Got it?"

Lucky moved toward him. "Then keep your eyes closed, jerk."

Varsity swore again and pushed Lucky with both hands.

Lucky staggered two steps away, then lunged forward and returned the shove. Varsity went back hard. He plowed into the Edgies behind him, and a couple of them went down. I would have been amazed at Lucky's strength if I hadn't been standing next to Trash. His grunt told me what had really happened—he'd given Varsity a little extra push.

A couple of the Edgies slipped toward the back of the mob. We were still outnumbered, but the odds were getting better.

"You asked for it," Varsity said as he scrambled to his feet. He pulled off his jacket and threw it to the ground. It landed where I could read the name written across the back. *Walden.* I guess that was his last name.

"Kick his butt, Walden," a kid in the mob said.

"Yeah, stomp on his face," another kid shouted.

I still didn't like the odds. If Lucky won, the rest of the kids might jump him. If he lost, they'd probably jump us. If we ran, they were close enough to catch us. It was time for a show of force.

As they told us in school: *Act like a criminal and people will treat you like one.* I stepped up next to Lucky and spat out the first lie that came to mind. "Hey, I'm already doing time for assault. What's a few more years?" I figured, with our reputation, they might think I really was dangerous. I did my best to look mean.

"Gonna have your hands full," Flinch said, stepping next to me. He leaned forward, putting his face close to Walden. "But I don't think I have anything to worry about. You probably punch like a little old lady." He turned his head away from Walden and grinned at us.

Walden threw a sucker punch, trying to hit Flinch when he wasn't looking.

Needless to say, Flinch's head was nowhere near Walden's fist.

"Missed, granny," Flinch said as Walden spun halfway around in his attempt to smash what wasn't there.

Torchie headed for the woods. Oh man, if he ran, we were doomed. Any sign of weakness and the mob would rush us. I was about to call after him when he returned, clutching a thick stick. He stepped next to Flinch, holding the stick at both ends. I could see a glowing spot in the center on the side nearest Flinch. I had no idea what he planned to do with a burning stick. He turned to his right and nodded to Cheater.

"What's he doing?" I whispered to Lucky.

Lucky shrugged.

Walden looked over his shoulder. His buddies were all hanging back. "Come on," he urged. "Let's kick some butt."

None of them moved.

Cheater stepped next to Torchie. He threw up his hands like a karate master. I thought he was going to chop the stick, splitting it with his hand. But he didn't do that. Instead, he paused, glanced at Trash, then at Torchie, and pointed up in the air over Torchie's head. Trash smiled and nodded.

Torchie raised the stick, holding it high over his head, still grasping it with one hand at each end.

Cheater crouched, then leaped. Trash grunted again, pushing Cheater higher in the air. As Cheater flew up, he shouted, "Hiyaaaa!" and snapped out a kick. The stick split with a sharp crack, breaking right where Torchie had burned it. As the pieces twirled through the air, two of the kids in the mob ran away.

Trash leaped forward, slashing out with the edge of his right hand. He hit one of the pieces as it fell. The piece flew like it had been blasted from a cannon. It shot across the street in a high arc, sailing over the cars that were parked along the other side of the road.

The night fell dead quiet as everyone watched. Nobody moved or breathed until the stick crashed through the front window of a house across the street. The sound of breaking glass is one of the few things on earth that can send any kid scurrying.

The Edgies took off.

Walden was right there with them. He didn't even stop to grab his jacket.

Between the performance we'd put on and the fear of getting blamed for the window, I guess they'd decided it was a good idea to leave the scene. So did we. As the porch light went on in the house across the street, we raced to the woods and headed into the pipe.

"We were awesome," Flinch said. "What a team."

"That was so cool," Torchie said. "I knew Cheater would figure out what I was thinking about chopping the stick. But I never would have thought up the kick part. That was so great."

"Yeah, nice move with the stick," Lucky said. "You, too, Trash."

"Nice and stupid," Trash said. "I almost broke my hand when I hit it. But it was worth it to see their faces."

"Yeah," I said. "I don't think we're going to get any more trouble from Edgies."

We pushed aside the manhole cover and climbed up to the school yard. I never thought I'd view it as a safe harbor. At the moment, I was glad to be back.

Between our victory over the Edgies and our smashing success at pinball, we were one happy crowd as we went toward the back wall.

"Me first," Cheater said, rushing to the ladder.

"Sssshhhh," I warned. "Someone will hear us."

"Who cares?" Torchie asked. "We're the champs."

"Champs!" Lucky shouted.

"Alters forever!" I yelled.

We all rushed at the ladder and started wrestling, getting wet and white and half frozen in the remaining snow. We ended up in a laughing, hitting tangle, with nobody trying seriously to go back up to Lucky's room. Finally, we all collapsed on the ground.

"We'd better get back inside," I said when I'd caught my breath.

"Winners first," Flinch said, pointing to Trash.

Trash shook his head. "No, that's okay. You take the lead, my man."

Flinch smiled, got up from the ground, shoved his trophy under his belt, and grabbed the ladder. He was more than halfway up the side of the building when he froze. An instant later, I froze, too, as I saw a head pop out from Lucky's window high above us.

"Look what we have here," Bloodbath said, his grin gleaming in the moonlight like a dagger of ice.

NEWSPAPER ADS IN MR. LANGHORN'S DESK DRAWER

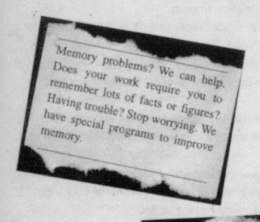

Memory problems? We can help. Does your work require you to remember lots of facts or figures? Having trouble? Stop worrying. We have special programs to improve memory.

Redland Phobia Clinic—we specialize in fear of flying. Let us help you conquer your problems. Don't let your fears keep you from experiencing the joys of travel. Call today for an appointment.

A DECLARATION OF WAR

The most awful part for me, standing on the ground, was watching Flinch as he tried to scramble down the ladder. I knew he must have seen what was going to happen before it happened. But there was nothing he could do. He was too far up.

"Have a nice trip," Bloodbath called. He leaned back and lifted his foot.

A loud snap shot through the winter silence. My stomach lurched as I realized Bloodbath had broken the stick that held the ladder in the window. Unlike when Cheater had broken the branch, this wasn't a harmless trick. The ropes, stretched tight a moment before, turned limp and useless. Flinch fell. The fall seemed to take forever, but for that whole dreadful stretch of nightmare time, I couldn't move. In my mind, I tried frantically to think of some way to help, to catch Flinch or break his fall. In front of my eyes, he tumbled away from the wall, his hands out in front of him like someone trying to hold off a monster. But the monster was the Earth. And nothing he did could hold it off.

The sound Flinch made when he hit was hardly more than a dull thump, muffled by the snow. But it jolted through me from my groin straight up to my guts.

We rushed over.

Flinch was sprawled on the ground. Oh man—he looked like a football player who'd just been hit so hard you knew he wasn't getting up.

I knelt next to him, but I had no idea what to do.

Torchie reached out and touched Flinch's shoulder. "Flinch. Hey. You okay?"

There was a faint sound. Crazy as the thought was, it reminded me of a chicken clucking. I listened more closely and realized it was Flinch, swearing quietly, saying the same word over and over.

"Flinch?" I asked.

He turned his head toward me. "Hurts . . ."

"Don't move," Torchie told him.

Flinch shook his head. "Freezing . . ." He reached out with his left hand. I grabbed it and held still, letting him raise himself. I was afraid I'd hurt him if I pulled. Flinch staggered to his feet, pieces of the broken trophy falling from his belt. His right arm dangled at his side, the hand twisted at an angle I didn't want to think about.

I looked up at the window. "We've got to get you taken care of."

"Don't want you in trouble . . ." Flinch said, gritting out the words through what must have been a terrible amount of pain. "They find out . . . no more trips . . ."

"Don't worry about it." I helped him walk around the building.

Torchie went to grab the ladder, then caught up with us.

Trash tried to open the front door. It was locked. There was no way we could get in without waking somebody.

"We have to knock," I said.

Trash shook his head. He stood there for a moment with his fists clenched. I heard a soft click. Then Trash reached up again and opened the door.

We got Flinch inside and up to the second floor. "Lie here," I told him. "I'll say you fell down the steps going to the bathroom. The rest of you get back upstairs."

Flinch nodded, then gasped something.

"What?" I asked, leaning closer to him.

"Snow," he said, pointing to my pants.

I brushed myself off, then got as much snow off Flinch as I could

without hurting him. I was about to go for help when Flinch spoke again.

"Jackets," he said.

"What?" I asked. Then I realized what he meant. I took off my jacket, then helped him with his. As careful as I was, I knew I hurt him when I slipped his right arm out of the sleeve. I tossed the jackets up toward the top of the steps. Then I rushed to see who had night duty.

It was Mr. Briggs. Before he could start thinking I'd come by for company, counseling, or a pleasant conversation, I told him, "Flinch fell down the stairs."

As soon as Mr. Briggs saw Flinch he said, "I'd better stay with him. Go back to my room and call an ambulance." He knelt next to Flinch, put a hand on his shoulder, and told him, "Hang in there. . . ."

When I got back from Mr. Briggs's room, I saw Lucky watching from the top of the steps. He ducked away when the men came with the stretcher.

After they took Flinch to the hospital, I went back to the room to tell the others what had happened. None of the rest of us could sleep. We sat in the room and waited. All of us were pretty wound up, but Lucky was the worst. He kept pacing back and forth. The way he acted reminded me of my dad every time he tried to quit smoking. After about an hour of pacing, Lucky dashed out of the room.

"What's up with him?" Torchie asked.

"No idea," I said. Though I had a suspicion.

Lucky returned a couple minutes later. He stopped pacing, but he looked really strange. Nobody asked him what was going on. Nobody said much of anything.

Early the next morning, Flinch got back from the hospital. His arm was in a cast.

"Broken?" I asked.

He nodded.

"This is war," Lucky said.

"Yeah," I agreed with him. "It's time to pay Bloodbath back."

"How?" Torchie asked.

"I don't know," I said. "But sooner or later, we'll get a chance."

That chance came sooner than I'd expected.

FEELINGS AND THOUGHTS

PRISCILLA NOMAD

Here in The garden ThaT was and is my mind

I find a rose, a flower. BuT oh iT's so unkind.

Sharp Thorn, such pain.

NoT just once, buT again.

Can I dare To feel my ThoughTs and Think my feelings?

Or must I siT and stare aT empty ceilings?

POLITICS

Saturday afternoon, I got fetched down to Principal Davis's office. I guess he wanted information about Flinch's accident. I wasn't happy about sitting there. Waiting to see the principal was no big deal—it was a fairly common experience for me—and sticking with the story was no problem. But I wasn't alone. Bloodbath was there, too, waiting his turn and casually peeling strips of vinyl from the back of the chair next to him. Five other seats were also filled. From what I'd seen, Davis caught up with discipline on the weekends. I guess he didn't have any hobbies at home.

"Whatcha do?" Bloodbath asked, glancing toward me without the faintest sign of recognition. I realized he had no idea I'd been in the yard last night. He didn't know, or care, who'd been outside that window. He didn't care who he hurt. I wanted to grab him and shout, *I'm here because you almost killed my friend!* But that wouldn't do any good.

There was no reason to make him suspicious. As much as I hated the idea of talking with him, I decided the best approach would be to act naturally. "Got in trouble with Parsons yesterday," I told him, selecting a safe reply. "You?" I figured that if I kept him distracted, he wouldn't grow bored with the chair and decide to start peeling pieces off of me instead. I really wanted to hit him, but I knew I'd never get away with that.

He shrugged. "I wrote my name in the wrong place."

"On a desk?" I asked.

"Nah, on some runt's face." He laughed, producing a sound I thought could only come from a baboon. He reached into his pants pocket and pulled out a marking pen. "Want me to show you?"

"No thanks." I fought the urge to switch seats.

He uncapped the pen, releasing a strong chemical odor into the air. "You sure?"

I could see it was one of those pens with the ink that didn't come off. This was getting out of hand. I had to get Bloodbath's mind away from using my forehead for a sketch pad.

Behind Principal Davis's door, a phone rang. A minute later, I heard the phone being slammed down.

"Ridiculous. They're moving up the inspection—because of pressure from the town. They can't do this to us! We were supposed to have the rest of the year. We aren't ready. They're coming this Friday."

Bloodbath and I both turned toward Principal Davis's door. It was him shouting. No mistaking that voice. I heard another familiar voice— Mr. Langhorn. Maybe they were having their shouters' club meeting.

"I thought the mayor was on our side," Mr. Langhorn said.

"Not anymore," Principal Davis said. "Apparently Mayor Walden changed his mind. I just found out he's been on the phone all morning calling in favors."

"Walden has a lot of powerful friends," Mr. Langhorn said.

"Oh crap," I muttered, seeing an image of that jacket on the street. *Walden*. We'd picked a fight with the mayor's son. Worse, he left his jacket right across the street from where we'd broken that window. One way or another, he was going to tell his father that the school was involved. Even if he had no proof, he could cause trouble.

"If they want to move the date, there's nothing we can do about it," Langhorn said. "Let's hope they like what they see."

"If they don't, they'll approve the merger plan," Principal Davis said. "I heard they're looking at a building in Riverside Junction. It'll save money, and that's all they care about. Pack everyone together in one huge mess of a school. You know they'll have more students for each teacher. Half of us will be out of a job when that happens. The worst part is, they don't care about the students. We're the only ones who really care."

I listened to the rest of it. A few minutes later, Principal Davis stepped out from his office. "Go away," he said. "I've got other problems. I'll deal with all of you later." He and Langhorn walked down the hall.

"Cool," Bloodbath said. He slipped out of the chair and headed for the outer door of the office. As he was leaving, he glanced back at me and said, "Guess this is our chance to bring Edgeview down. One huge mess of a school. That's what Davis said. Sounds like my kind of place."

Bring the place down? I didn't like the sound of that. I waited until I was sure Bloodbath was far enough away so he wouldn't change his mind about writing his name on my head. Then I hurried upstairs and told the others what I'd heard.

"What's that have to do with us?" Torchie asked.

"If Bloodbath wants something, we want the opposite. No matter what. If Bloodbath wants to screw up the inspection, then we want the school to pass," I said. I didn't tell them the part about the mayor's son. They were so proud about standing up for themselves, I couldn't let them know that we were probably the reason the inspection was rescheduled.

"Why should we care about the school?" Lucky asked.

"Because we don't know where we'll end up if they close Edgeview," I said. "It could be some big place. They're talking about Riverside Junction. That's real far from here. Your parents might not come for you as often. That's not all. We might get split up. They could put us in different classes. Different rooms. How'd you like to end up with Bloodbath or Grunge for a roommate? How'd you like to have a bunch of teachers like Mr. Langhorn? It could happen. This place might be hell, but at least it's our hell. We have to stop Bloodbath."

There was silence in the room for a moment as that sunk in.

"You really want to stop Bloodbath, don't you, Martin?" Torchie asked.

"Yeah."

Torchie nodded. "Then I guess that's what we want, too."

"But who knows what they might try?" Flinch asked.

"Right," Lucky said. "Who knows?"

At that moment, all the rest of us turned toward Cheater. "Who knows?" we all said. Then we all shouted the answer. "Cheater knows!"

"What?" Cheater said.

"You can find out their plans," I told him. "Then we can stop them."

"It sounds kind of dangerous," Cheater said. "How can we stop Bloodbath and his gang? They're too tough."

"We're smarter."

I looked over at the source of those words.

Trash spoke quietly from his seat on the floor. "Between us, we've got a lot more brains than those thugs. And we have a few secrets. Watch this."

WHY I LIKE BEING ME

EDDIE THALMAYER

I'm sorry this is late, but I didn't feel like doing it before. Anyhow, I guess I like being me because I'm a good artist. I really like to draw. It feels good to create something new. It feels bad to destroy things. When I pick up my pen and start drawing on a blank piece of paper, I know I can make something wonderful.

LOST AND FOUND

*T*rash stared at Torchie's desk, one corner of his mouth still turned up in a grin. Torchie's notebook rose slowly and gracefully into the air. Then it opened and the pages started to turn, one by one. Three pencils floated up to join the book, each drifting in a different pattern. All three pencils moved to the paper and began drawing. My jaw dropped as I watched. The demonstration only lasted for about twenty seconds. Then the notebook shot straight up, slamming into the ceiling so hard that little chips of paint dropped down. The pencils spun across the room. Two of them bounced off the wall while the third stuck point-first, quivering in the plaster. Everything else ended up on the floor.

"Oops," Trash said. "Still a bit rough at all of this. Guess I need more practice."

"Looks like you've been practicing a lot," I said. This went far beyond just throwing stuff.

Trash shrugged and grinned.

"So you think we can do it?" Flinch asked me. "Do you really think we can beat Bloodbath?"

"Sure. We'll figure something out." I realized that the others were looking toward me as the leader. That was a mistake. But I'd step aside as soon as I figured out who should really take charge. "We have less than a week. The inspection is on Friday."

The rest of the day passed quietly. We spent most of the time in the room. With all of us urging him to find out what he could, Cheater looked for a way to get close to Bloodbath, but he didn't come up with anything. Trash worked so hard on his talents he reminded me of a warrior training for combat. Torchie practiced his fire control. Flinch killed time describing various ways he could use his cast to rearrange Bloodbath's face. Lucky didn't say much, but he did wander into the halls once in a while, usually returning with an object or two he'd found. I watched the five of them and wished I was really part of the group.

Sunday afternoon, when Lucky didn't come to the room, I went down the hall to see him.

"What's up?" I asked.

He was sitting on his bed, staring at something. He raised his hand to show me what he had.

"Oh no." I took the wallet from him and flipped it open. My gut tightened as I recognized the picture on the driver's license. I didn't even have to read the name. "Where'd you get this?" I asked, handing it back to him.

"I found it on the steps," he said.

I remembered how Lucky had gone out while we were waiting for Flinch to come back from the hospital. The wallet must have fallen from Mr. Briggs's pocket when he was kneeling down to help Flinch. "You have to return it," I said as I handed it back to him.

Lucky shook his head. "They'll nail me," he said. "Or throw me in jail."

I'd figured there was something he hadn't told us about his power. "You hear stuff, right? That's how you find things."

"I'm not crazy," Lucky said.

"I never said you were. Tell me about it. Do you hear the things you find?"

Lucky nodded. "Lost objects, mostly. Sometimes hidden things, too. They whisper to me. If I pick them up, the voices stop. If I don't, they get louder."

"Well, just put the wallet where he'll find it," I said.

Lucky shook his head. "If I do that, the voices will drive me crazy. Once I pick something up, I can't put it back or toss it away. I've tried. When I do, it starts screaming at me. All I can do is keep it or give it to someone."

"Give it to me." I held my hand out.

"You going to give it back to Mr. Briggs?" he asked.

"Yeah. I'll take care of it." I took the wallet from him and put it in my pocket. I figured I could slip it in Mr. Briggs's desk. Or I could toss it in the garbage. I didn't owe Mr. Briggs anything. Either way, Lucky would be in the clear.

"Thanks," Lucky said.

We sat and talked. Mostly Lucky talked and I listened. He was terrified of being locked up. That's why he never told anyone about the voices. At least now he knew he wasn't crazy.

The bell rang for dinner.

Right after we got to our table, Principal Davis walked in. "Your attention, please," he said. "I've just been informed that at some point this weekend, a wallet was stolen from Mr. Briggs. This sort of behavior will not be tolerated at Edgeview. Fortunately, I have a very good idea who the culprit is. It would be best if he returned the wallet immediately."

I thought about dropping the wallet on the floor. That wouldn't work. It would be right next to us. I could tell them I'd found it, but then they'd ask why I hadn't returned it before.

Before I could figure out what to do, Principal Davis came over to Lucky and said, "Very well, Dominic. It looks like you want to do this the hard way. Come with me, please. Perhaps we need to arrange for you to spend some time in the company of other criminals."

"But . . ." Lucky spread his hands in a display of innocence.

"Come with me now, please," Principal Davis said. He grabbed Lucky's arm and pulled him from his chair.

Lucky looked back at me, his eyes pleading. I stood, planning to shout, *Wait!* But the words caught in my throat. I didn't want to switch places with Lucky. I didn't want Principal Davis dragging me off.

"He's dead," Cheater said. "Even his dad won't get him off this time."

"No." I headed out of the cafeteria. Whatever else I'd done wrong, I wasn't going to add this to my list. But I couldn't face Principal Davis. I ran up the stairs, hoping Mr. Briggs was still on duty.

"Martin," he said when he answered my knock, "this is getting to be a tradition. I hope you aren't here to tell me about another injury."

"You dropped this Friday," I said, holding out the wallet. "Principal Davis thinks Lucky—I mean Dominic—stole it. He didn't."

Mr. Briggs took the wallet from me.

Neither of us spoke. I waited for him to say something. He just looked at me.

"I didn't steal it either," I said.

He didn't answer. Okay, I could play that game, too. I stared back. Sooner or later, he'd have to say something.

Finally, he spoke. "How would you like me to treat you, Martin?"

"What?" That took me by surprise.

He put the wallet in his pocket. "I don't have a clue. Not a clue. It's like you're waving me closer with one hand and slashing a knife with the other. I believe you didn't take the wallet. Beyond that, I don't know what to think."

I moved a step away from him.

"Well, I'd better rescue your friend from Principal Davis." He closed his door and walked down the hall.

How would you like me to treat you? What kind of a question was that? "I don't want to be treated like anything," I shouted. But he was gone by then.

I went back to the cafeteria. Before the meal was over, Lucky came in. "You took your time," he said.

"Sorry."

"Don't worry about it. If I'd been in your spot, I'd probably have left town."

"So we're cool?" I asked.

Lucky nodded. "I can't blame you for freezing."

"Will someone tell me what's going on?" Torchie asked.

We filled him in, then headed up to the room.

When classes started Monday morning, it was easy to tell that something was happening. The teachers were all nervous. The funny thing was that they were all nervous in different ways. Mr. Langhorn got even angrier and shouted more than before. I thought he was going to break something inside his head the way he was yelling at us. I could just imagine his head flying apart like a watermelon with a stick of dynamite inside of it. Miss Nomad, impossible as it might seem, got even more disgustingly nice, like she was hoping to soften us up. Mr. Briggs just acted kind of distracted.

It was also obvious that Bloodbath and his gang were planning to cause trouble. In a way this was actually good because they spent less time than usual terrorizing the rest of us. It looked like they were saving their energy for something grander.

There was only one incident before the inspection, but it was a whopper.

ALPHRAX CHEMICAL CORPORATION

Dear Mr. Briggs:

While reviewing our files, your application and resume came to my attention. While the position you applied for last year was filled internally, I am extremely impressed by your qualifications. It would be my pleasure to offer you an interview for the position of senior lab manager for our East Coast division. Please contact me at your earliest convenience so we might arrange a meeting that suits your schedule.

Sincerely,

Harlan Watterstone

Harlan Watterstone
CEO, Alphrax Chemical Corporation

BLOW UP

*B*ack in sixth grade when I'd been an astronomy nut, I'd learned this neat word: syzygy. It's what they call it when several heavenly bodies line up. But syzygy can be bad news when earthly bodies are involved. Torchie found that out on Wednesday. We were walking along the first-floor hall right after lunch. Torchie was ahead of me. Down the hall, someone had left the door open on one of the broom closets. Hindenburg was ahead of us. He'd stopped near the closet to tie his shoe. The sight of his gas-filled butt pointing in my direction was enough to slow me down, but Torchie kept walking. Right when Torchie reached the closet, Bloodbath came along in the opposite direction. The three of them—Torchie, Hindenburg, and Bloodbath—were lined up perfectly with the open closet.

Syzygy.

Bloodbath took one look at the two of them and I guess he just grabbed the opportunity. He charged into Torchie, knocking him into Hindenburg and pushing both of them into the closet. Then he slammed the door shut and leaned against it.

"Hey!" Torchie yelled from inside. He started pounding on the door. I wanted to help him, but I wasn't sure what I could do.

"Come on," Torchie shouted. "I'm dying in here."

"Gas chamber," Bloodbath said.

Kids clustered around, getting close enough to see what was going on, but not so close that Bloodbath could reach out and snag them.

"Please!" Torchie wailed. "Let me out. I can't breathe." He pounded on the door.

I heard a louder crash. It sounded like Torchie was kicking the door. Two more kicks jarred the door. I took a step closer, then stopped as I realized the danger of Torchie, the human flame, trapped in a closet with Hindenburg, the human gas tank. I turned and raced away.

An instant later, along with the smash of the loudest kick yet, a huge WHUMPF of an explosion ripped the air. I glanced over my shoulder in time to see the door go flying, pushing Bloodbath across the hall. Too bad it hadn't flattened him. I'd have loved to have seen him knocked on his butt.

Bloodbath took off, strolling down the hall as if he'd had nothing to do with the destruction.

Torchie staggered out, gasping, as the smell of the world's largest lit fart rolled through the hall. It was a good thing the inspection wasn't today. The smell alone would have been enough to close the school forever. Behind Torchie, Hindenburg stumbled out, looking dazed.

"You okay?" I asked Torchie.

"It was awful. . . ."

"I can imagine." We hurried off to class.

"We're going to get that guy, aren't we?" Torchie asked as we reached Mr. Briggs's classroom.

"You bet." I tried to sound confident. I really wanted to score a few points for our side. That was all I thought about for the rest of the day.

"Have you learned anything?" I asked Cheater that evening. The inspection was only two days away.

He shook his head. "It's not that easy. I told you, I get stuff people are thinking, but it's not like reading a book. I can't just look into someone's mind. I guess it's more like a radio. You know, like when you're in a car and you start scanning through the stations."

"Maybe if you got closer to them," I suggested.

"Good idea," Torchie said.

"That's easy for you to say," Cheater told him. "If you got in trouble with them, you could just set something on fire. I don't have any way to protect myself. I'm not going near those guys. I'm the kind of person they like tossing around. In case you hadn't noticed, Bloodbath isn't just mean and violent and ignorant. He's also prejudiced."

"I've noticed," Flinch said. "I think we've all noticed."

"You want to get sent somewhere else?" I asked.

Cheater shook his head.

"Do you trust us?" I asked him.

Cheater paused for a second, then nodded. "Yeah."

"Will you take a bit of a risk?" I asked.

"I guess," Cheater said. Then he asked me a question. "Do you have any idea what you are doing?"

I shook my head. "Not a clue."

ESPIONAGE

"Okay," I asked the group, "how do we get Cheater close to Bloodbath?"

"Without getting me killed," Cheater added.

"I know," Lucky said. "Torchie could start a fire. And then when everyone comes running to see what happened, that would give Cheater a chance to sneak up behind Bloodbath."

"Too dangerous," Torchie said. "I'm just starting to get control."

"Yeah," Flinch said, "and if there was a fire, they might accidentally serve us a hot meal."

"But some kind of distraction isn't a bad idea." I turned to Trash. "Could you make some noise at lunch?"

"I guess," Trash said. "I could make some trays fall off a table or something like that."

I nodded. "That would do the trick. When everyone is looking, Cheater can sneak up behind Bloodbath and try to figure out what's in his mind."

"I know what's in his mind," Flinch said. "Nothing. Blankness. Empty space. The final frontier. Zip. Diddly squat."

"There's *something* rattling around in there," Torchie said.

"Yeah," Lucky agreed. "I've heard it rattling."

"I'll do it," Cheater said. "But I'm not sure if it's right."

That surprised me. "What's wrong with listening in on someone's thoughts?" I asked.

"Well, it's kind of like spying," Cheater said.

I hadn't looked at it that way. I guess people have a right to keep their thoughts secret. This was a special case, though. "It's for a good cause," I said. "Right?"

"Yeah," Cheater agreed, "I suppose so."

"Hey, if I could read minds, I'd be thinking about how I could use my power to rule the world," I said.

"You sound like a cartoon character," Lucky told me.

Flinch nodded. "Martin Mindmaster, Conqueror of the Universe."

Lucky started laughing. "With his faithful sidekick, Zucchini, who can read the minds of vegetables and fruits."

Things pretty much collapsed after that. We didn't spend any more time working on our plan. The guys were too busy making fun of me. But I figured Trash would give it his best shot, and that was all I could ask.

The next day, as we took our seats at lunch, nobody was joking around. "You ready?" I asked Cheater.

"No, but I guess that doesn't matter." He got up from the table, then looked at Trash. In a voice like someone from a bad western movie, he said, "Cover me."

Trash nodded and turned so he could watch Cheater's path around the room. Cheater hugged the walls as he made his way over to Bloodbath's table. Then Trash focused his attention toward a table of the runts. One of the runts slammed his fist down on the table. At that very instant, his tray flew up. It was almost breathtaking—the silverware and dishes seemed to dance in the air as they shot above the tray. Each piece took its own path, arcing still higher, then falling toward the ground like spray from a silver water fountain.

"Wow," I whispered, wishing I could do that. Trash really was an artist.

Everyone looked over. I snuck a glimpse at Cheater as he rushed up behind Bloodbath. Cheater's face was scrunched up so much I wondered whether he was grunting. Bloodbath, and the rest of the kids at his table, were all standing to get a better look at the action.

I heard another tray launch. There were shouts of protest from the runts' table. Cheater was still in place. Trash launched a third tray, then slumped back, breathing like he was exhausted.

"Oh no," I said, looking back at Bloodbath. He seemed to have lost interest in the flying trays. He'd sat back down, then started to glance over his shoulder. When Bloodbath saw who was behind him, it would be Cheater who'd get tossed up in the air like a piece of silverware.

Trash groaned like he was lifting something heavy. A spoon catapulted from a bowl of pudding in front of the kid opposite Bloodbath. It hit Bloodbath right in the middle of the forehead. For an instant, the spoon hung in place, glued to Bloodbath's head by the legendary sticking power of cafeteria tapioca. Then it slid down and fell to his tray.

Cheater managed to get away as Bloodbath struck back at the kid opposite him and a food fight broke out. He scurried over to us.

"Well?" I asked.

"I picked up something about candles."

"What about them?" I asked.

He shook his head. "It didn't make sense. *Thirty minutes for a candle.* I wish I knew what that meant."

"Well," Lucky said, "that was a waste of time."

I looked over at Bloodbath's table. "I don't know. It's kind of nice to see him with a face full of pudding."

Several teachers came in and broke things up. Nobody got punished. At Edgeview, a small food fight was nothing. No bones had been broken. No faces had been smashed.

"Now what?" Lucky asked as we left the lunchroom.

I shrugged. "I wish I knew."

In science class after lunch, Mr. Briggs was the first teacher to mention anything about the inspectors. "Listen, class," he said, "there are going to be some people here tomorrow to observe our school in action."

"Yeah, action . . ." I heard Bloodbath whisper to one of his buddies.

That drew some snickers and laughs from the back of the room.

Mr. Briggs kept talking. "The important thing is for all of you to act the same way you would if nobody was watching. Just be yourselves. I'd appreciate it. And I'm sure the rest of the staff would, too."

One of the runts raised his hand. "Yes, Michael, what is it?" Mr. Briggs asked.

"I heard they're going to close Edgeview. Is that true?"

"They just want to see how well we're doing things," Mr. Briggs said. "If they feel we aren't giving you the best education you can get, they might want to make some changes. Even if they decide to make changes, it won't happen overnight. These things take time."

He left it at that. But I knew my life was due for another jolt if the inspection didn't go well. I hung back in the room as the period ended and everyone else filtered out into the hall.

"What is it, Martin?" Mr. Briggs asked.

I wasn't sure. I wanted to say something nice, but I was afraid it would sound phony. So I asked about something that was on my mind, even though I didn't expect any real answer. "The school," I said. "I don't know if it's a good place or a bad place."

"Few things are that simple." Mr. Briggs stopped and ran his hand through his hair, then took a deep breath. "I don't know if I should tell you this," he said, "but you'd probably figure it out sooner or later. Maybe you already figured it out."

"What?" I had no idea what he meant.

"Edgeview isn't just the last stop for students."

I still didn't get what he was talking about. Instead of explaining, Mr. Briggs gave me his patented you-figure-it-out look.

It hit me. *Not just us.* Them, too. "Teachers . . ." I said. Mr. Briggs nodded. Then he smiled an embarrassed grin. "I've been kicked out of more than one school, too, Martin. Not for being bad. I just have my own ideas about how to teach. The people who run schools don't always like that. They don't like the way I dress." He glanced down at his Penn State T-shirt and jeans. "They don't like the way I teach.

Sometimes, they don't like the way I think."

"So you've kind of gotten into trouble, too," I said. The thought made me smile.

Mr. Briggs nodded.

"What about the rest of them?" I asked. "Are they all here for that kind of reason?"

He shook his head. "I can't speak for them. But I don't think Edgeview was anyone's first choice."

"Not even Miss Nomad?" I asked.

He chuckled. "Maybe she's an exception. But that doesn't mean we aren't all trying our best. Not one teacher here is giving you anything less than his best efforts. You might not think so, but I promise it's true."

"It must be tough," I said, "ending up in a place like this when you don't want to be here."

"Who said I don't?" Mr. Briggs stared out the window for a minute. "Maybe, at first, I felt I was getting shoved into Edgeview. But now that I'm here, I feel good. I feel good about the work I'm doing, and I feel good about myself. That's important." He held out his hand. "Whatever happens, it's been a pleasure."

It felt strange to shake his hand. I dropped it after the briefest instant. For once, I had nothing to say. I hurried out to my next class.

That evening, as we hung out in the room, we tried to think of anything else we could do, but we were out of ideas. So we ended up sitting around talking about other stuff.

I realized I'd really miss these guys if the school was closed. They were my friends. And here, at least, you were only considered abnormal if you didn't get into trouble. Maybe this was where I belonged. Maybe I'd been lying to myself about my behavior. When I'd first met Torchie, I'd thought he was the one who couldn't see how bad he was. Funny how things change.

"We'll just have to do our best tomorrow," I told them as the group broke up for the night.

"Our best can be pretty good," Flinch said.

I smiled as I watched him leave the room. He was right. Our best really could be good.

Memo From: Principal Davis
To: All Edgeview Faculty
Subject: State Inspection

I know we discussed these issues in last evening's meeting, but I can't emphasize how crucial it is to keep control of the students during this inspection. While the inspectors have surely met students with various disciplinary problems, I don't think they are prepared for the worst of our residents. With that in mind, please make a special effort in the following areas.

1. Despite the cold weather, please be sure to leave at least two windows open in any classroom occupied by Waylon Grestman.

2. If at all possible, avoid any conversation with Martin Anderson. As I'm sure you all know, he seems to thrive on abusing his instructors. For this one day, try to ignore him.

3. Make a special effort to keep the small students away from the large ones. We don't want a repeat of last year's human volleyball game, especially not when there are inspectors present.

Together, I know we can show them what a fine institution this is.

INSPECTION

I was awakened by the sound of tires crunching gravel against frozen ground. I watched from the window as they spilled out of their car near the front door. Six of them. From my high, sharp angle, I couldn't tell much about the inspectors.

They were in the cafeteria at breakfast—a half dozen men and women wearing business clothes and carrying clipboards. It was like a third life-form had invaded our strange little planet of teachers and students. They stood near one wall, watching us and whispering among themselves.

"Any idea what they're thinking?" I asked Cheater.

"Not from this far away. But look at them. I get the feeling a couple of them are scared of us," he said.

"Scared of us?" That idea surprised me. I knew the Edgies were frightened by our reputation, but those Edgies were just kids. These were adults. It never occurred to me that adults would be afraid of kids. I wondered how they'd feel if they knew some of the kids had amazing powers.

"Bloodbath is being pretty quiet," Lucky said.

I glanced over toward Bloodbath's table. Lucky was right. A gang of them was just sitting there eating breakfast. Nobody was wrestling or shouting. "I bet they're saving their energy for something big," I said.

Grunge came in late and joined Bloodbath. Then two more of the gang came strutting into the cafeteria and nodded at Bloodbath as they took their seats. He grinned and nodded back. A moment later, the bell rang for class.

"They're planning something," I said. "See if you can pick up anything," I told Cheater.

I expected him to protest that it was too dangerous. But he surprised me. "I'll try," he said. He wove through the crowd and managed to slip behind Bloodbath for a moment. Then he had to back off as they got closer to the door. I guess Cheater didn't want to get trapped next to him in a crush of kids.

"Well?" I asked Cheater when he'd worked his way back to me.

"Twenty candles," he said. "I just got that thought in my mind. *Twenty candles, all set to go.*"

"Candles, again. Any idea what it means?" I asked.

Cheater shook his head. "Not a clue."

"Hey, check this out," Lucky called. He opened a closet door in the hallway just outside the cafeteria and pointed at something. "Look what I found."

"What the heck . . . ?" Torchie asked.

I looked inside at the lit candle. It was stuck on a small square of wood—probably jammed onto a nail. A fuse was wrapped around the base of the candle. The other end of the fuse led to a shorter fuse coming out of a large cardboard tube.

"That's an M-8o," Cheater said. "Big-time firecracker."

I unwrapped the fuse from the candle. "They must have used the candle so it would go off later, when everyone was in class. That way there'd be no chance of getting caught."

Torchie bent over and blew out the flame. "Don't they know it's dangerous to leave a fire going like that?"

Lucky grabbed the M-8o and put it in his pocket, then dashed down the hall to the next closet. He opened the door and waved for us.

"Oh man, that's bad news," I said. This one had two M-8os attached to a candle. But that wasn't the worst part. The explosives were taped against the side of a water pipe. If they blew, the place would get flooded. Even for Bloodbath, that was an incredibly stupid and dangerous stunt.

"Bloodbath must have done this," Lucky said. "At least we found it before it went off. Think there are any others?"

"Twenty candles!" Cheater shouted. "That's what they were thinking. They must be spread all around the school. If even one goes off, it could do a lot of damage."

"Can you find the rest of them?" Torchie asked Lucky.

"I don't know," Lucky said. "I don't think I can search for something specific. I just find stuff. I can't control what I find."

"There's no time, anyhow," I said. I grabbed Torchie by the shoulder. "You're our best bet. You've been learning how you start fires. Do you think you can put them out, too?"

"Uh . . . I don't know."

"You have to try," I said. "That's the only way. Do your best."

Torchie nodded. Then he got this blank look on his face. I had a sudden horrible fear that he'd get it backwards and turn the whole school into a blazing bonfire instead of putting out all of the candles. I was struck by images of the walls around me bursting into flames. Talk about making a bad impression on the inspectors. *Welcome to Edgeview. Watch us burn.*

Torchie stared off into the distance. A drop of sweat ran down his forehead. I waited for something more dramatic. I expected him to at least grunt or groan or pass out. But finally, he grinned and said, "I think I did it."

"How can we tell?" Lucky asked.

"If you don't hear the place blowing up all around us, you'll know it worked," I said.

We hurried along the hall. As I sat in math, I kept bracing for an explosion. It never came. By the end of the period, I was pretty sure Torchie had succeeded.

We'd won the first battle. But I had no idea what else Bloodbath might do.

On the way to our next class, Lucky found two more of the M-8os. Both candles had gone out. "You did it," I told Torchie, patting him on the back. "That's great."

"Yeah, guess I did. I think putting all those fires out helped me, too," he said. "The more I understand what I can do, the better I can learn to control it."

I noticed wisps of smoke coming from his notebook. "Uh, Torchie," I said, pointing to a smoldering spot next to his index finger, "this might be a good time to work on that control."

"Oops," he said, dropping the notebook. But instead of stomping on it, he just got that blank look for a moment and the fire went out.

As we reached our next class, I saw that Bloodbath didn't deal well with frustration. He knocked a couple of the runts out of his way as he came into the room. The rest of them scattered like mice scooting from the path of a lawn mower.

Up near the front of the classroom, a woman in a gray suit wrote a note on a small pad. I wondered whether Bloodbath might be able to do enough damage even without the explosions.

Next to me, Cheater snapped the tip of his pencil. He got up and walked to the back of the room toward the sharpener, taking the route nobody ever took—going right past Bloodbath. I thought it was pretty brave of him, especially since he caught a quick punch on the arm as he went by. When he returned to his seat he glanced toward Bloodbath, then whispered, "Lunch. He's planning something for lunchtime."

There was nothing I could do right now. In the meantime, I tried to pay attention in class. The funny thing was, I didn't get a chance to give the inspectors a good impression. None of my teachers called on me.

The rest of the morning, things were pretty quiet. As I walked toward the lunchroom, I wondered how long our good luck would hold.

DINNER CONVERSATION AT THE ANDERSONS'

Dorothy Anderson: Maybe we should drive out to Edgeview this Saturday and visit Martin. Or maybe even bring him home for the weekend.

Richard Anderson: What's the point? We'll just have a miserable time. If I want abuse, I can get as much as I want at work. I don't need to spend two or three hours in a car for that.

Dorothy Anderson: But I'm sure he misses us.

Richard Anderson: Him? I doubt it.

Dorothy Anderson: Really, Richard, you shouldn't be so—

Richard Anderson: Don't you start. I have enough people telling me what to do.

Dorothy Anderson: But—

Richard Anderson: Just drop it.

CONFRONTATION

*A*ny idea what they're planning?" I asked Cheater when we reached our table. We'd gotten sandwiches today. Apparently, there'd been some problems with the ovens. They'd all gone out right before first period. I guess Torchie really had doused every fire in the place. At least the workers had noticed the problem before the place filled with gas.

"Rumble," Cheater said.

I glanced over to Bloodbath's table. He was talking to a whole bunch of thugs who clustered around him. "He's not that stupid," I said. "If he starts a riot in front of the inspectors, he'll just get tossed out of here. No reason for us to stop him. Life at Edgeview would be almost bearable without Bloodbath."

As I spoke, a couple of the thugs left their group. They each sat down at a different table. More of them did the same thing, spreading around the cafeteria.

"I think they're going to start a bunch of fights," Flinch said.

"Oh no," Torchie said. "Look who's headed here."

Bloodbath, the last to get up, had left his table. He was heading right toward us. I looked around. His gang was spread out among the tables. Even Lip had picked a spot—with the smallest of the runts, of course.

Maybe it was stupid of him to split up his group. But even with the six of us against him, I didn't want to tangle with Bloodbath.

"Any ideas?" I asked the guys at the table.

That's when I noticed Trash. He was staring at Grunge, who was at the table to our left. Trash's teeth were clenched. He had a look on his face like—well, there's no polite way to put it—he looked like someone who hadn't been able to go to the bathroom in three or four days and was trying to get it over with real hard. After a moment, he switched his attention to another of the thugs.

"Hey," Torchie said, "watcha doing, Trash?"

"Sshhhhh," I said. "Let him concentrate."

"Hello, friends," Bloodbath said. "Mind if I join you?" He dropped into a seat between Cheater and Torchie, grinned at us, then glanced at the clock on the wall. Cheater raised his hands up in fists and flashed his fingers opened and closed. He did it twice. Twenty. That's what he was telling me.

I checked the clock. It was seventeen minutes after twelve. I figured Bloodbath had picked a time when they'd all leap into action. Twenty after.

I tensed, getting ready for the fight. Maybe I could jump on him before he really hurt Cheater. If I grabbed his arms, I might be able to slow him down until he shook me off.

Tick. The clock moved to twelve-eighteen.

Trash lowered his head. He seemed to be staring under the table.

"Hey," Bloodbath said, looking across the table at Trash. "What's wrong with you?"

"Leave him alone," I said. I had no idea what Trash was doing, but this was no time to let him be disturbed.

Tick.

Twelve-nineteen.

"Guess what? You're about to get hurt," Bloodbath said. "All of you. And it's going to be a pleasure."

I stared back, ready to dive at him when the clock ticked. He didn't know that I knew. Maybe that would make a difference. I just hoped

Cheater figured out that he needed to run for the door.

Time crawled. I could almost feel the seconds trudging past. I thought of those dying flies that drag themselves across the ceiling at the start of winter.

Tick.

Bloodbath leaped from his seat and lunged toward Cheater to his right. He tried to lunge, that is. As his body snapped to a halt, he got the weirdest look on his face. So did the rest of his gang. They all fell down at once.

I'd already jumped out of my chair. Now, as I stood there, braced to leap to Cheater's defense, I realized there wasn't going to be a fight. The table jerked as Bloodbath yanked his leg. I peeked around, already suspecting what had happened. Bloodbath's sneaker lace was tied around one of the legs that jutted from the base of the table.

Bloodbath was swearing in frustration now. Principal Davis and the teachers had run over to the flailing thugs. They got the kids back on their feet and tried to lead them from the room. The whole group was stuck until someone suggested they remove their sneakers.

"Wow, good work," I said, looking over at Trash. "It was you, wasn't it?"

"Yeah." He nodded. His voice was barely above a whisper. He looked pretty wiped out.

For a moment, his eyes flickered. I reached toward him, afraid he was going to pass out. But he shook his head hard once, then opened his eyes all the way. I thought about the old Trash, beaten down by the world. He was nothing but a memory. "That was really cool," I said. I reached out and clasped his shoulder.

Trash smiled. "Thanks."

Across the room, the inspectors were all sitting at a table, talking to each other. Several of them kept glancing at their watches, even though there was a clock on the wall. "Looks like a good spot for you, Cheater," I said.

Cheater got up and sighed. "It'll be a lot less terrifying than getting close to Bloodbath."

He walked over to the inspectors' table. "Excuse me," he said, "do you have any salt?" Then he leaned between two of them, reaching for the salt. He grabbed the shaker and walked back toward us, staggering like someone who had just run face-first into a lamppost.

"Wow," he said, shaking his head hard.

"What?" I asked. "Did you get anything?"

He dropped back into his chair. "I'll tell you, adults sure have a lot of junk rushing through their heads. Give me a minute."

I waited while Cheater sat with his eyes closed. Finally, he took a deep breath and opened his eyes. "Okay. According to what I picked up, two of them want to recommend that the state should close Edgeview, two want it to stay open, and the other two haven't made up their minds yet. They're almost done with everything on their list. The final thing they want to do is to talk to a typical student. After that, they'll make their final decision."

"Just one student?" Flinch asked. "What's the point?"

Cheater shrugged. "They have to get back to the capital for a meeting. They don't have time to talk to a lot of kids. They figured one would be better than none. Actually, you can learn a lot more than you'd expect from a small sample properly chosen from a large group."

"So, it could all depend on who they pick and what he says." I looked around the cafeteria at the mass of trouble that passed for students at Edgeview. "We're dead."

"Any idea who they're planning to talk to?" Lucky asked.

Cheater shook his head. "I don't know."

That's when Principal Davis returned to the cafeteria. He went over to the inspectors and handed them a stack of paper. One of the inspectors pulled out a sheet from the stack. He passed it to the woman next to him. She closed her eyes and stabbed at it with her finger, then said something to Principal Davis. As he leaned over her shoulder and looked down at the paper, his expression changed. He frowned and shook his head. His face reminded me of someone who'd just lost a big bet. He scanned the cafeteria, then he headed toward our table. *What did I do this time?* I wondered. Principal Davis came right up to me. "Martin . . ."

"Yes?"

"I really wish it was someone else—just about anyone else—but our guests would like to speak with you after lunch."

"Me?" I really couldn't believe this.

"Unfortunately. I would have suggested someone more pleasant, but they picked you. Come to the office when the bell rings."

I was too stunned to say anything. I just sat there and watched him walk away. *Anyone but me,* I thought. All I had to do was spend ten minutes in a room with the inspectors and they'd probably decide to call in an air strike to wipe Edgeview off the map. At the very least, they'd probably boot me out immediately, no matter what the regulations might be.

"Do you really care what happens to Edgeview?" Lucky asked me.

I thought about Principal Davis and his punishments. I thought about Mr. Parsons and his anger. But I also thought about Mr. Briggs and his passion for teaching. And Miss Nomad, who cared too much. And Ms. Crenshaw, who tried to make classes interesting. And I thought about all the kids who needed some place in the system. I nodded.

A strange smile flitted across Lucky's lips. "Personally, I wouldn't bother. But if that's what you want, then it's time to use your power, Martin."

FROM A DRAFT OF A REPORT BY
DR. LENORE HARPER ON THE STATUS OF
THE STATE'S ALTERNATIVE SCHOOLS

The minimal success of the current alternative schools leaves us with a tough decision. There seem to be three available choices:

1. Leave the system in place for another five-year test period. Advantage: the staff will gain experience. Disadvantage: the system has done little to improve the drop-out rate or address the needs of these students.

2. Merge the four existing schools into one program. A suitable building is available. Advantage: this move will save money. Disadvantage: some parents will have to travel a greater distance to visit their children.

3. Abandon the alternative school approach. Advantage: substantial savings that can be spent elsewhere. Disadvantage: there's no place else for these students to go.

TALENT

The statement was so strange, I didn't even react to it for a moment. Finally, I said, "What are you talking about? I don't have any power."

Lucky snorted out a laugh. "Hey—where have I heard that before? It sure sounds familiar. We didn't admit our own powers until you forced us to accept the truth. It's the same with you. You have a talent, too. You can't see yours. But we sure can."

"That's crazy," I told him.

"There's that word again. You know I don't like it." He shook his head. "I'll ask you the same question you asked us. *Why are you here?*"

"Because I got kicked out of a bunch of other schools," I said.

"But *why*?" Lucky asked.

"I talk back. You know that. I've got a smart mouth."

"Big deal. A lot of kids talk back," Lucky said. "Just about every kid on the planet talks back. But you go way beyond that. You have a gift. You know how to hurt someone. You know how to dig deep and hit a nerve."

"It's like Torchie's grandfather," Flinch said. "The one he told us about who always pats him where he's hurting. Except you do your hurting with words. Whether you mean to or not, you always hit the target."

"Crazy," I said again.

Lucky reached out and grabbed both my shoulders, then leaned forward and put his face right in front of mine. "You hate this, Martin. You hate having someone in your face—especially an adult. And when someone gets too close, you hit him hard. That's your talent. You know where it hurts."

"Stop it." I tried to pull away.

"No. Say some painful words, Martin. Hurt me. Prove it. I'm in your face. You hate this. Let me have it. Cut my heart out." He leaned so close his forehead butted up against mine.

I jerked against his grip, but he held on, his fingers digging into my shoulder muscles. I stared at a face that was so close I couldn't even focus on it, hating the feel of his hot breath washing over me. The words shot out. "You're pretty cocky for a kid who still wets his bed."

I felt the fingers go loose. Lucky jerked away from me.

"I'm sorry," I said. I didn't know where those words had come from, but I'd have given anything I owned for a chance to take them back. "I didn't mean—"

Lucky swallowed hard, and his cheeks grew red. "That's . . . okay . . . It doesn't matter. I had to prove it to you."

"Is that true?" Torchie asked.

"Shut up," Flinch said to him.

I knew, by the look on Lucky's face, that it was true. He'd risked humiliation to show me that I had some sort of power. Even so, I didn't want to believe him. I wanted to pound his face with my fists and scream that he was wrong.

"Your power is pretty obvious," Cheater added. "Once we figured it out, it was really amazing watching you in action."

"No . . ." I tried to protest. But in my heart, I knew anything I said would be a lie. My world had been yanked on its side. Or flipped inside out. The past flooded over me, all those times I'd lashed out. All the pain I'd caused. Striking. Slashing. A thousand injured faces littered the trail of destruction I'd carved.

"Cheer up," Cheater said. "You're one of us."

He was right. I had a hidden talent—my very own psychic power. Wonderful. What a great gift. I could jab a knife of words into anyone's heart. I couldn't see how that would make any difference right now. What good was the power to make people angry? "I don't get it," I said. "This won't help."

"Use your power in reverse," Flinch said. "Just like Torchie did when he put out a fire. Instead of finding the thing that hurts the most, find the thing that makes the person feel good."

This was almost too much for me. "I don't know if I can."

"You'll have to," Torchie said.

The bell rang. Lunch was over.

Dear Mr. Watterstone:

I am deeply flattered by your letter. Alphrax Chemical Corporation has a wonderful reputation. Much to my surprise, I realize that I am happy being where I am, and doing what I'm doing. Many thanks for the job offer, but I must regretfully decline.

While I have your attention, let me add that our school is always short of funds. So if you have any old lab equipment or supplies you'd care to donate to a worthy cause, I can assure you we'll put the material to good use.

Sincerely,

Dale Briggs

Dale Briggs

MEETING

*I*n prison movies, they talk about the long walk—that's the one-way stroll the guy takes from his cell to the electric chair. I was taking a long walk from the lunchroom to the principal's office.

My mind was a blur of thoughts. I had a power. I still only half believed it. It was wonderful and terrible at the same time. And it almost had to be true. How else could I have managed to so deeply annoy so many teachers? Not to mention my parents and just about every other adult who'd ever tried to get close to me.

Lucky had proved it. He'd allowed me to humiliate him in front of the others. Lucky, who in his way was as fiercely proud as Cheater, had done this for me. Whether he cared about Edgeview or not, I had to try to do this for him and for all the rest of them. And for myself.

Could I reverse my power? Could I make someone feel good? I reached the end of the hall and put my hand on the doorknob. Another question caught my attention. Was it right? Was it okay for me to use this power to get what I wanted?

I'd told Cheater it was okay.

But was it?

I stepped into the office. Principal Davis was waiting for me. "Nice shirt," I said, trying to tell him something that would make him feel good.

He frowned and ignored my comment. I realized it had been a poor attempt. I hadn't looked into his deepest fears and hopes, I'd just blurted out a dumb compliment.

"In there," he said, stepping away before I had a chance to get close to him and try again. "And for heaven's sake, try to be something other than an annoying little monster for once in your life."

I walked into the room and found the inspectors seated around a table. "Come in," a man in a brown suit said. "Have a seat." He was wearing a bow tie. Wonderful.

"Thanks." I pulled out a chair and sat down, then tried to figure out who was in charge. The leader seemed to be the woman across the table—the one in the gray suit.

"Hello, Martin," she said as she held out her hand. "I'm Dr. Harper."

"Hi." I reached out and took her hand. As our fingers met, I knew what I wanted to say. The knowledge stunned me for a moment. Oh man. It was sitting right in my head. I'd actually seen her deepest failure. She'd spent years trying to get a job with a textbook company, but they kept turning her down. The words formed in my mind. *Well, you may never make it to the book company, but you're probably skilled enough to get a job at a miserable rat hole like Edgeview.*

I actually bit my tongue—not hard, but enough to keep the words from spilling out. Dr. Harper gave me an odd look. I realized I was still holding her hand. I let go. As our fingers drew apart, I realized something else. She'd wanted to have children. That was her deepest desire. Past that, I glimpsed one other image buried within her. She was proud of her eyes. She was smart and serious and dedicated and hardworking. But she was also very human and very proud of her eyes.

Other words came to mind, replacing the attack I had almost unleashed. *Gee, you have nice eyes. They're just like my mom's.* It would be so easy. If I said that, she'd have to like me. With the right words, I could get her to do whatever I wanted. I knew for sure I could control her. There wasn't the slightest doubt in my mind.

A tingle ran through my scalp.

"So, Martin," Dr. Harper said, "tell us what it's like for you at

Edgeview. Don't be shy. Tell us everything you think is important. We want to know what's good and what's bad about your school."

I looked around the table. They all sat ready with their pens and clipboards, waiting to hear me speak. The man to my left was close enough that I knew his deepest sorrows and desires. The same for the man on the right. It would be so easy. If I wanted to, I could become their favorite kid in the world just by telling them the things they needed to hear. They'd love me. I'd own them. I faced the woman with the beautiful eyes.

I started talking.

I spent nearly half an hour in that room. When I left, I found Principal Davis pacing in the outer office. "What did you say?" he asked.

"The truth."

"Well, I might as well pack up and leave." He groaned and hurried into the room with the inspectors. As the door closed behind him, I could hear his nervous chatter. "Now, remember, that's just one student. There are dozens of wonderful kids here. Martin can be a bit abrasive at times. He's actually one of our most difficult cases. Don't let that bother you."

I left the office. Bloodbath and a couple of his gang were lined up on chairs just inside the door. I guess Principal Davis wanted to talk with them. I walked past, trying not to catch anyone's eye.

As I went down the hall, I heard footsteps. Two pairs. Following me. One big and heavy pair of feet, one small pair. I walked toward the stairs. The footsteps sped up. Before I got to the steps, Bloodbath reached me, grabbed my shoulder, and spun me around.

"You bastard," he said, grabbing me by the shirt. He shoved me against the wall.

WHY I LIKE BEING ME

L. BLOODBATH

From Lester Bloodbath's wastebasket:

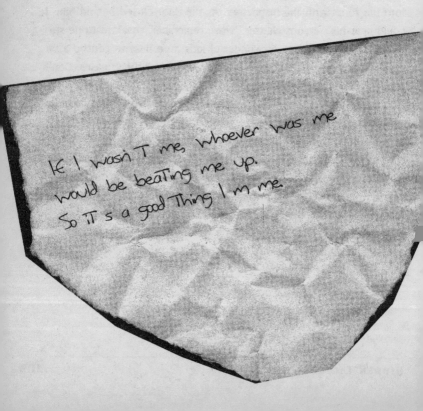

If I wasn't me, whoever was me
would be beating me up.
So it's a good thing I'm me.

SHOWDOWN

*W*hat?" I asked, looking desperately around, hoping to spot a teacher. There was no sign of help. The halls were empty.

Bloodbath turned his wrists and dug his knuckles hard into my collarbone. "I don't know how you did it. But it was you. I've seen you with those freaks. You ruined everything. Now I'm going to ruin your face."

Behind him, Lip laughed like a crazed hyena. Panic nearly shut down my mind, but I fought against it and used the only weapon I could. I stared at Bloodbath and I knew the darkest fears inside his dark heart. I pointed at Lip. "You going to let him laugh at you that way?" I glanced toward Lip, still bracing for the punch from Bloodbath that would snap my ribs like dry spaghetti. "Man, you shouldn't laugh at him like that, Lip. Don't you have any respect?"

Bloodbath glared at Lip and loosened his grip on my shirt. Lip stood, his mouth open. My words must have caught him so much by surprise that he couldn't think up a response. His silence looked like an admission of guilt. Maybe part of what I'd said was true. It didn't matter. Just as long as Bloodbath thought it was true. I knew, as only I could know, that Bloodbath hated the merest hint that someone might laugh at him. I didn't know how it started. I didn't know where or why. But I knew that this was his one gigantic button—the sore, unhealed wound. This was what you pressed to set him off. To laugh at Lester Bloodbath was to die.

Lip was doomed.

I could slip down the hall and flee to safety while Bloodbath was kicking the crap out of his pathetic little shadow. Bloodbath reached out and grabbed Lip by the arm. He raised a fist.

No. This wasn't the way it should be.

"Let him go," I said. "How stupid are you? He wasn't laughing at you." I shook my head. "What an idiot. You are a true moron, Lester." Then I laughed at him. I whooped and roared with all I had in me, striking him with a mocking cackle that echoed through the halls.

I must have been an idiot.

Bloodbath tossed Lip aside. He whirled back at me. Lip bounced off the opposite wall, staggered, caught his balance, then scurried away. There was nothing for me to do but put up a fight. Even so, I figured I was going to end up with a lot more broken bones than Flinch had gotten.

Bloodbath charged at me, pulling back his right fist for a punch. The look in his face—it was the look of a bully who was about to do damage. It was the look of a bully about to feast on pain.

A jolt ripped through my gut. It wasn't fear. Fear wasn't in the hallway. I was jolted by Bloodbath's expression. I'd seen that same look so often on my father's face. The face of a bully. All my life, I'd lied to myself. I'd pretended it was something else. But my father had whipped me like a dog, only he'd done it with words. And, bully that he was, he'd enjoyed it.

Rage guided me. I shot out my own right fist. It connected straight with Bloodbath's jaw. I don't know which of us was more surprised.

Bloodbath dropped so fast it looked like he'd been anchored to the floor with rubber bands. I froze, waiting for the aftershock of our collision. Slowly, I realized that the fight—this fight, at least—was over.

Unbelievable. No, very believable, I realized as the answer came to me. "Flinch . . ." I whispered. All those hours throwing punches. All that practice. I'd developed one heck of a right hook. It had sure made an impression on Bloodbath. He was stretched flat out on his back, his eyes clouded like those of a dead fish. A low moan escaped his lips, along with a trickle of spit. Maybe he'd never been hit before. Probably not. Who would have dared to?

Who, indeed?

Resisting the urge to step on Bloodbath's chest, I walked past him. Lip stared at me from around the corner, his eyes so wide they reminded me of Ping-Pong balls.

"Have a nice day," I said. I turned away from Lip and headed upstairs toward my class. I was just in time for the end of science.

"Well," Cheater asked as I plopped down on the rug, "did you get them angry?"

"Nope," I said.

"So you said nice things to them?" Torchie asked.

I shook my head. "Not that, either."

"You didn't use your power?" Lucky asked.

"I didn't use it, and I didn't let it use me. I took another route. I just told them the truth."

"And what would that be?" Lucky asked.

"The truth is that Edgeview isn't a bad idea, but the teachers could do a lot better job if the really dangerous kids were sent someplace else. Not everyone who's here should be here. I told them that most of us just wanted to learn and to fit in, but that it was hard when there was a small gang of bullies who terrorized the rest of us."

"That's it?" Torchie asked.

I shook my head. "Nope. I told them one other thing. There had to be a way to get out. There always had to be hope, no matter how long someone had been here. One chance at an evaluation isn't enough. Let a kid prove he's ready to go back to his own school. After a month, after six months or a year. Whenever he feels he's ready, he should have the chance."

Lucky sighed. "I hope they listen to you about the bullies."

They did.

A week later, Bloodbath and most of his gang got transferred. I'm not sure if it was to another school or just some kind of detention place. Maybe they all just got sent home. It didn't matter, as long as they were gone. As Bloodbath was leaving, Flinch started dancing in front of him, calling him names. Bloodbath tried to hit him, but Flinch just kept ducking and dodging. After every dodge, he'd reach out and tap Bloodbath on the face with his left hand. Just light taps. He didn't sock him with the cast on his right hand. After a while, Bloodbath looked like one of those boxers who's gotten way out of shape and shouldn't be fighting. He was panting and gasping. I almost felt sorry for him. Almost.

We went up to the room so we could watch from the window as Bloodbath and his buddies were loaded onto a bus. I smiled when I recognized the driver. He'd keep that group under control.

"There's one thing I don't get," Torchie said after the bus had pulled out of sight.

"What's that?"

"Why did you ask them to set up a way out? I mean, we don't want to break up. You don't want to leave us."

I didn't answer him right away.

"Martin," Cheater said. "You don't want to go away, do you?"

"I think you already know the answer to that," I said.

"Maybe Cheater does," Torchie said. "But I sure don't."

"You've been great," I said. "All of you. You're the first real friends I've had. But my family . . . All these years, I've really screwed things up."

"Tell me about it," Torchie said. "I did the same thing. There isn't a piece of furniture in the whole house without burn marks."

"You should see my place," Trash said.

I nodded, thinking about some of the more awful moments from the past. "I almost can't blame my dad for hating me." I gasped as my own words sunk in, squeezing my chest into a tight knot. For a minute, I couldn't talk. I'd never admitted that particular truth before.

"It's time to try to fix things," I said. "I could hide here. It would be easy. But I can't. I have to go home. Maybe there's no way to get Dad to like me. I don't know. But at least I can be there for my sister."

Torchie nodded.

"It takes at least a month to go through all the steps," Cheater said. "That's what I heard. So at least you'll be around that long."

"And we'll have fun," Lucky said.

"Lots of fun," Trash said. He floated a handful of quarters out of Lucky's pocket and dropped one in front of each of us.

"Oh yeah," I said, looking at my friends. "We'll have fun. This is going to be a month to remember."

And it was.

FORM 2937-A EDGEVIEW SCHOOL

STUDENT RELEASE FORM

Student Name: Martin Anderson

The undersigned assert that the student in question has successfully completed the evaluation process as described in state guideline #355287 and has been judged ready and capable of returning to a school in his home district.

EPILOGUE

*I*t took me a bit more than two months to get out of Edgeview. Old habits are hard to break. But I showed them, finally, that I was fit to return to a regular school. I got out in the middle of May. The school year was almost over. Part of me wanted to wait and finish out the year at Edgeview, but I guess I knew the time had come to move on. It was good to get home. My sister Teri made dinner for me the night I got back. It must have been rough for her while I was away. She looked terrible when I first saw her. But Dad got off her back as soon as he had me around for a target.

I'd hoped he'd be less angry, now that I was acting better. But he almost seemed annoyed that he didn't have anything to get mad about. I don't know if I'll ever get things straightened out between us. But if I fail, at least I'll know it's not all my fault. Maybe he'd have been no different even if I'd never talked back. There's no way to find out. And no real point in wondering.

The guys write me all the time, telling me what's going on in their lives. I write back, of course. Trash sends me drawings. He's really got a gift for art. Flinch sends me jokes. It wouldn't surprise me if he ended up on television one of these days. Lucky sends me all kinds of little stuff. In his last note, he told me he's learning to handle the voices and not pick up anything that will get him in trouble.

Cheater sends me trivia questions and logic puzzles through E-mail.

Once in a while Torchie sends me a tape of himself playing the harmonica. He really is getting pretty decent. They all decided to try to leave Edgeview, too. That's good. They don't belong there.

Every once in a while, I get a postcard from Mr. Briggs. Just for fun, I sent him a T-shirt from the local college. Their mascot is a duck. I hope he wears it to the next staff meeting. I can just imagine the face Principal Davis will make.

Each day is a bit of a struggle. I still have to fight to keep from getting people angry. I mess up a lot, but I'm getting better. And, on top of that, I have to wrestle with the urge to make them do what I want by telling them what they want to hear. Sometimes I slip. I'm human.

But I've decided it's okay to use my talent to make people feel good, as long as I'm not doing it because I want something from them. I guess it's my way of making up for getting so many people angry. The last thing I want is to be a bully. Not all bullies use their fists. Some use words.

It's not easy. I imagine every talent has a price, both the talents we know about and the hidden talents—the gifts we haven't yet discovered.